TO LAUGH

LAURA SCOTT

READSCAPE PUBLISHING, LLC

CHAPTER ONE

Jonas McNally slid out from behind the wheel, then leaned heavily against his car, staring up at his grandparents' large and cheerful yellow house. It felt good to return to the place filled with happy childhood memories.

The bright warm sunshine and the blue Michigan water were the same. The only thing missing was the laughter.

At least on his part. Maybe the B&B guests would find the joy that eluded him over the past few months. The house looked exactly the same as he remembered when he and his siblings had spent summers here. The McNally Mansion as it was known by the townspeople. The place was still regal, tall and proud, the way his grandparents had been. It was sad that his grandparents had passed away while he'd been overseas, but it was good that Jazz and Jemma had created a business that would honor their memory. He and his three brothers had been more than willing to add their support to the twins' business endeavor.

With a sigh, he braced himself on the car, hopping on one foot until he could open the rear passenger door to pull out his crutches. The three-hour drive from the VA hospital in Battle Creek, Michigan, had been grueling. Seven weeks since his injury and his left leg throbbed like a bad toothache, amplified by a thousand.

Tucking the crutches under his arms, he gingerly made his way across the wide parking area toward the front door. He was a day early because he'd left the VA hospital against medical advice. The only thing that would help him now was physical therapy. He knew it. The doctors knew it. Why they resisted signing his discharge paperwork was beyond him. He was fed up to his eyeballs with bureaucratic bull.

Getting acclimated into the civilian life was what he was supposed to be doing, right? Here was the place to start. He lifted his hand and rapped on the door. Hopefully, his twin sisters wouldn't mind his unexpected early arrival.

"Coming!" A cheerful voice reached his ears. The door opened revealing his sister Jemma, her blond hair pulled back in a bouncy ponytail. She gasped in surprise. "Jonas! You're here!"

"Yep." He tried to smile but thought it probably looked more like a pained grimace. "Hope it's okay."

"You're always welcome." Jemma quickly embraced him, enveloping him in the scent of cinnamon and cloves. When she stepped back, her gaze dropped to the spot where his left foot was supposed to be. "Oh, Jonas." Her voice was full of regret and sympathy. "Why didn't you tell me? Tell any of us? We would have been there for you."

"Hey, I'm alive. That's what matters." He hated the way people stared at his now deformed left leg. And he wasn't here to get sympathy from Jemma or anyone else in the family. "You gonna move out of the way, or what?"

"Of course!" Jemma's cheeks went pink, and he inwardly winced, realizing his curt sarcasm had hurt. It had been too long since he cared about other people's feelings. She opened the door, holding it with one arm so he would have room to maneuver. "Please come in. Are you hungry? Thirsty? What can I get you?"

"I'm fine." His appetite had vanished with his left foot, but there was no need for her to know. He was afraid she and Jazz would hover over him as it was. He swept his gaze around the great room, settling in on the oil painting depicting the Cliffs of Moher in Ireland. His grandmother had painted it from memory shortly after she and his grandfather had immigrated here.

Once he'd dabbled in painting, but that was a long time ago. Before the Army. Before Afghanistan. When he'd still had two legs and no flashbacks.

Another lifetime.

"What do you think?" Jemma asked, her tone uncertain as he took in the great room.

"It's just like when we were kids, down to the cherry wood furniture. I can't believe it all looks the same."

"Grandma and Grandpa took good care of the place." Jemma shut the door behind him. "Come into the kitchen. There isn't a family room any longer; we're using that space for the dining area."

He crutched after her, taking in the changes she'd mentioned. He was sad that he wouldn't be able to sit in the family room to watch the lake but understood why they'd chosen to offer that view for their guests. Upon reaching the table, he propped the crutches in the corner and then gingerly sat down. "How's business?"

"Great!" Jemma's brown eyes lit up with excitement. "Thanks to several amazing reviews we're finally beginning to get noticed. We have two weddings booked, three if you count Jazz and Dalton's upcoming ceremony."

"Where is the bride to be?"

Jemma sent him a concerned look. "Didn't you hear the sounds of hammering and sawing? They've been working on fixing up a small apartment for me and Trey over the garage."

Every muscle in his body went still, then he abruptly stood and reached for the crutches. "I didn't hear anything."

"Jonas, no!"

He ignored her, moving fast despite his disability. Something was wrong. Fearing the worst, he threw open the door, trapping it with one crutch as he angled his way back outside.

Stepping out on the porch, he came to an abrupt halt when he saw his sister and a dark-haired guy climbing out of her cherry red truck holding two pizza boxes. The truck was parked next to his boring four-door sedan. It still galled him that he'd had to give up his yellow Mustang convertible, but driving a five-speed manual transmission was impossible when you only had one foot.

"Jonas!" Jazz thrust the pizza at Dalton before rushing over to throw her arms around him. If she noticed the crutches or his missing limb, she didn't let on. "It's so good to see you."

"Back at you." Pinching the crutch under his armpit, he patted her back. "Hey. Introduce me, sis."

"Oh!" She let him go and stepped back, subtly swiping dampness from her cheeks. "Jonas, I'd like you to meet my fiancé, Dalton O'Brien. Dalton, this is the youngest of my four older brothers, Jonas."

"Nice to meet you, Jonas." To his credit, Dalton's gaze didn't linger on his injury. The guy stepped forward and offered his hand. "I want you to know I love your sister very much."

Jonas shook his hand, appreciating Dalton's directness.

"Glad to hear it. You should know if you hurt her, I'll have to hurt you."

"Jonas." Jazz rolled her eyes. "You're not my father."

"I would do the same thing in your shoes," Dalton said, ignoring his fiancée and holding Jonas's gaze. Jonas appreciated the sign of respect.

"I may not be her father or the oldest brother, but I am here to protect her. I understand you're getting married."

"Yes. Jazz wanted to wait for you. Now that we've set the date, the rest of the brothers have promised to be here, too."

"Even Jake is flying in from Ireland," Jazz added. "We haven't seen him since Grandma's funeral."

The funerals he'd missed. Granddad had died first, then Grandma three months later. Jemma came out of the house to join them. He sensed the look between his twin sisters but ignored it.

He was already dreading seeing the expression on his brothers' faces when they noticed his missing leg. He turned to look at the large four-car garage. He'd been so focused on the house that he hadn't noticed the new windows framed in on the upper level.

"You're creating an apartment up there?"

"For Jemma and Trey, and eventually Garth."

Casting his mind back, he placed the name. The guy who'd answered Jemma's phone the night he'd decided to let her know he was in the hospital.

"We're engaged," Jemma said with a shy smile. "He's a great guy, Jonas. You'll meet him later tonight."

"Sounds good." The joy reflected on his twin sisters' faces was blinding. He was truly happy for them.

But being surrounded by this much cheerfulness was already wearing him down. Jonas decided then that he'd only stay long enough to watch Jazz and Dalton get married, before blowing out of there.

No sense in dragging down the rest of the family as he worked through his issues.

He was better off on his own.

～

Izabella Collins drove her car into the driveway of The McNallys' B&B. The place was impressive, better than she'd expected.

She hopped out of the car and then hauled her suitcase out of the back seat.

Inspired by the Irish name and the location overlooking Lake Michigan, Bella had chosen The McNallys' B&B as the place to stay for the next ten days. Ten days while the powers that be at the Battle Creek VA Hospital decided her fate.

Paid leave, they called it. A euphemism for getting together the evidence they needed to fire her. She hadn't done anything wrong, but it was her word against Dr. Hackbarth's and Emily's, his physician assistant. Hackbarth and Emily had claimed she was the one responsible for the error, despite the fact that Hackbarth had been the one to use the wrong antibiotic on the patient, causing the poor guy to go into anaphylactic shock resulting in a heart attack and subsequent death.

It still burned her britches that Eli Hackbarth had thrown her under the bus in order to cover his own butt. The jerk. Emily Archer had claimed Bella had given the antibiotic, too, even though the PA's back was turned and she couldn't possibly have seen anything unless she had eyes in the back of her head. Even the surgical tech in the room, Aaron Campbell, had claimed he hadn't seen Hackbarth provide the wrong medication.

The whole team had turned against her.

And to think she'd stayed late to help them out! So much for gratitude. Men were slime-buckets, each and every one of them. Whatever. She wasn't going to think about what had transpired.

As far as she was concerned, this was a paid vacation, courtesy of the Battle Creek VA. No dwelling on what the outcome of the investigation might be. She knew, only too well, how hospital administrators tended to support the doctors over their own nursing staff. At least when it came to a he-said, she-said scenario. And in this case, it was three against one.

Tugging on her suitcase with more force than was necessary, she made her way up to the front porch. Before she could knock, a pretty blonde opened the door.

"Ms. Izabella Collins? Welcome to The McNallys' Bed and Breakfast! I'm Jemma McNally, please come in."

"Thanks, but please, call me Bella." She hauled her suitcase up and over the threshold. Stepping into the great room was like taking a step back in time. "Wow, it's beautiful!"

Jemma beamed. "I can't take the credit, this used to be my grandparents' home. I hope you find it as comfortable and welcoming as we do. Here, I'll take your bag. You'll be staying in the rose room."

"Sounds awesome, but really, I can take my own luggage up. It's my fault for overpacking."

"No, please, I insist." Jemma reached for the bag, and they played tug-of-war for a moment before Bella relinquished her grip.

She followed Jemma up the sweeping grand staircase,

imagining how it must have looked in its heyday. Had the McNallys held parties in the great room? Had Jemma sat at the top of the stairs as a child, watching the events below?

"Here you go." Jemma sounded a bit breathless from the weight of Bella's suitcase. "I hope you like it."

"It's great." The room done in a relaxing shade of green was as quaint and perfect as the rest of the place. "And the view!" She crossed over to peer out at Lake Michigan. "Stunning."

"Again, I can't take any credit," Jemma said with a laugh. "This afternoon, I'm serving vanilla macadamia nut cookies along with coffee, tea, or lemonade, whichever you prefer."

"Herbal tea would be great." Bella turned away from the window. "No caffeine after noon for this girl."

"You and me, both," Jemma confided. "Head down whenever you're ready."

The idea of unpacking didn't appeal, so Bella washed up in the bathroom, then headed down the stairs. At the bottom she saw an incredibly handsome man on crutches coming out of the kitchen into the great room. She couldn't tear her gaze from the muscles of his upper arms and shoulders rippling as he maneuvered through the furniture.

"Hi." The greeting popped out of her mouth before she could stop herself. Was it any wonder her impulses sometimes got her into trouble? "I'm Bella Collins. Are you a guest here, too?"

The man's deep brown eyes burned into hers for a moment, before shying away. "Yeah, I guess you could say that."

"Great." She stood where she was, hoping he'd introduce himself, but of course, he didn't. She told herself to get over it. It wasn't as if she were looking for a man.

Slime-buckets, remember?

"Oh, Jonas, why don't you sit here for a few minutes with our guest? I have enough cookies for both of you." Jemma set the tray down near the sofa. "What would you like to drink, Jonas?"

The man with the crutches grunted as he lowered himself to the chair to the right. "Lemonade works."

"Great. Coming right up."

Bella sampled a vanilla macadamia nut cookie, moaning when it melted in her mouth. "This is incredible."

"Yeah. My sister has amazing baking skills."

It was the longest sentence he'd uttered. She glanced at him in surprise. "Jemma is your sister?"

He reached for a cookie. "Gee, you're a quick one, aren't you?"

She narrowed her gaze, not appreciating his sarcasm. "Yeah, that's me. The sharpest knife in the drawer."

The corner of his mouth quirked. Was that his idea of a smile? If so, it was pathetic.

Then again, with his shaggy blond hair and chiseled features, she suspected his smile might be lethal. Even wearing what appeared to be a perpetual scowl on his face, he was devastatingly handsome.

"Here you go." Jemma handed Jonas a tall glass of lemonade. The crisp lemony scent almost made her wish she'd chosen the lemonade over the herbal tea. Seeing Jemma and Jonas together, it was easy to see they were brother and sister in that they shared the same coloring including their blond hair and big brown eyes. "Jonas, I've put you in the yellow room, hope that's okay."

Jonas shrugged as if he didn't care. "Yeah, sure."

"I have a young couple celebrating their anniversary coming in this weekend, and I've placed them in the blue room." Jemma's smile was contagious as she took a seat beside her brother and helped herself to a cookie. She turned toward Bella. "The blue room is the closest thing we have to a honeymoon suite."

"Sounds lovely," Bella said. "I'm sure they'll enjoy it."

"Do you have any special plans for while you're here?" Jemma asked.

"Not really, although I can't wait to explore a bit. I just love small towns, don't you?"

"Mommy!" The sound of a child's voice sent Jemma to her feet.

"Coming, Trey." She smiled again at Bella. "Excuse me. I hope you enjoy your stay with us."

Jemma disappeared from the room, leaving her with grumpy-face.

"Did you grow up here?" Bella asked, unable to stand the suffocating silence.

"No." Jonas finished his cookie, then drank half the glass of lemonade. "Summers only."

Oookayy. The man was the antithesis of a chatterbox. "I bet it was a lot of fun. Do you have other brothers and sisters? Or is it just you and Jemma?"

He stared at her for a long moment, as if trying to decide if she was human or an alien from another planet. There were days she wasn't sure herself. "There are six of us," he finally said. "Do you always ask so many questions?"

"Me?" She thought about it for a moment. "Yes, I guess I do. I'm a naturally curious person."

"Nosy," he corrected.

She huffed, but then laughed. Hadn't her father often accused her of being too nosy for her own good? "I prefer curious."

"Aren't you afraid of ending up like the cat?"

She glanced around in confusion, then realized what he

meant. "That's just an old cliché. I'm fairly certain no cat was ever actually killed by curiosity."

He quirked an eyebrow but didn't say anything more. He ate a second cookie, but she restrained herself. She had no doubt that Jemma's baking skills would prove detrimental to her waistline.

"Well, that was excellent." She finished her chamomile tea, setting the cup aside. "Guess I'll see you around, Jonas."

The way he stared at her was a bit unnerving. She swiped a hand over her face, wondering if she had crumbs sticking to her cheeks or chin.

Bella pushed herself to her feet, disconcerted when he quickly stood as well. He grabbed for his crutches before she could offer to help, and she sensed he was standing out of sheer politeness. Someone had drilled some manners into the guy.

"Aren't you going to ask?"

Jonas's abrupt question caught her off guard. "Ask? About what?"

"My leg."

She held his challenging gaze, sensing this was some sort of odd test. "I assume you hurt it playing sports."

"Aren't you a pretty little liar." The words were spoken in a harsh guttural voice.

She reared back as if he'd slapped her. "Hey! There's no reason to be a slime-bucket."

"Slime-bucket?" he repeated. "Is that the best you can do?"

"What is your problem?" She was fast losing her patience with the guy. She hadn't paid any attention to why Jonas was on crutches, and she didn't really care. His injury, from whatever it was that he'd suffered, was none of her business. Thankfully, he wasn't her patient.

"Look at it," he commanded.

"Why?" She refused to bend to his will. "As a nurse, I'm no stranger to injuries. I can guarantee I've seen worse than whatever scar you're so anxious to show off."

"I doubt it," he said in a low tone. "I can only hope and pray you've never been exposed to the things I've seen."

It took a minute to realize what he meant. He was speaking as if he'd survived a war, and maybe he had. Jonas suddenly reminded her of the men she'd cared for at the VA hospital in Battle Creek.

But she knew better than to show him any sympathy. "Army? Navy? Air Force? Or Marines?"

"Army. Special forces."

She nodded, keeping her gaze on his face. It all made sense now. She didn't have to see his leg for herself to understand what must have happened. She knew, firsthand, how so many soldiers returned from being deployed missing one limb or more thanks to the plethora of hidden bombs the locals used to attack or defend themselves.

"Glad to see you made it out of there, alive."

Again, his gaze registered surprise. As if he'd expected something different. "Yeah. Thanks."

Bella hesitated, then said, "Ryan didn't."

"Didn't what?"

"Make it back. Ryan was my brother. He died in Afghanistan six months ago." She turned away. "See you later, Jonas."

She felt his gaze boring into her back but forced herself to ignore it.

Jonas had issues, so what? Didn't everyone? She had her own baggage. Her career was in shambles, which meant she might have to start over, somewhere. Doing what kind of nursing? She had no clue.

Regardless, the last thing she wanted to do was to become emotionally involved with a wounded soldier. Her brother wasn't the only one who didn't make it back home.

The man she'd hoped to marry hadn't returned either. The only thing she had left of Greg Wallace were photos and love letters.

Jonas McNally had no clue how fortunate he was.

CHAPTER TWO

She'd never once looked at his amputated leg.

Jonas stared after the pretty brunette trying to under-stand what had just happened. Other than the fact that he'd been a jerk and owed her an apology. Yet the way she'd snapped back had surprised him. He could believe she had a brother considering she'd refused to give an inch. It was sad to hear her brother had died overseas.

Most of the women he'd met since suffering his injury, okay sure, they were all nurses and physical therapists, had been kind and sympathetic, catering to his needs to the point he couldn't stand it.

But not Bella Collins. Oh, no. She acted as if she couldn't have cared less about what had happened to him. Not only did she refuse to give an ounce of sympathy, she'd gone on to remind him he was alive when her brother wasn't.

No one had dared talk to him like she did. Oddly enough, he found Bella's frank attitude refreshing. Slime-bucket? Hearing her call him that had nearly made him smile.

Something he hadn't done in the nearly two months since his injury.

He shook his head and used his crutches to navigate the grand staircase heading up to the second floor where the bedrooms were located.

The yellow room was awash with light, and the brightness was almost too much to bear. He found himself wishing he'd stayed in a motel rather than coming here to the family B&B. Too late to change his plans now, the twins would go crazy asking endless questions and poking their noses into his personal life.

Jazz's wedding couldn't come soon enough.

He glanced around the room, belatedly realizing he'd left his duffel bag in the sedan. Calling himself every kind of idiot, he clumped back down the stairs.

After weeks of being cooped up indoors, it felt good to be outside. Maybe he could hang out in the gazebo for a while and listen to the waves rolling across the lake. He crutched to his car, popped the trunk, and pulled out his large army issue duffel. After propping it against the vehicle, he slammed the trunk lid shut.

"Need a hand?"

Balancing on his crutches, he glanced over his shoulder to see Dalton crossing the parking lot toward him. "No thanks. I got it."

Dalton nodded. "Okay. If you feel up to it and have time to spare, we could use some help on the garage apartment."

Jonas narrowed his gaze, wondering if his future brother-in-law was joking. It was one thing to focus on being independent, but performing construction work on one leg? That was impossible. "Doubt I'll be much help."

"We need help screwing Sheetrock in place." Dalton

lifted a brow. "Looks to me like you can still wield a power drill."

It was on the tip of his tongue to lash out at the guy, but he managed to refrain. Bad enough that he'd taken his temper out on Jemma's guest. Bella had left the house and had driven away, heading toward town. He knew her abrupt departure was his fault.

He forced himself to consider the option—or challenge —Dalton had thrown at him. Helping to hang drywall was better than sitting around and feeling sorry for himself.

"Why not? Give me a minute to get my stuff inside and I'll see what I can do to help." Jonas hefted the duffel over his shoulder and then used his crutches to return to the house. The process took much longer than it should have because the duffel was heavy and shifted his balance.

He was sweating by the time he'd returned to the main level. Gritting his teeth against a sense of helplessness, there was nothing worse than feeling weak, he pushed himself to continue, crutching to the garage.

The staircase leading up to the second story looked sturdy enough. He clumped up the stairs using the crutches, one at a time; the sounds of hammering, drilling, and the twang of country music grew louder as he reached the top.

The space was bigger than he'd imagined, and they'd gotten pretty far along. The setup was basic but nice. There was an open-concept kitchen and living space along with two bedrooms with a bathroom tucked in between. The plumbing had already been done, as well as the electric. He could see just where the kitchen sink and the fridge would go.

"This place is really coming along," he said, raising his voice to be heard above the din.

"Yeah, it's getting there." Jazz set down her drill and

swiped her brow with her forearm. "Once we finish the drywall in the living and kitchen areas, we'll be on the homeward stretch."

Jonas nodded. "I can help."

"Great!" Jazz looked relieved. "That frees up Dalton to put in the toilet and sink in the bathroom."

He tried not to dwell on the simple things he couldn't do, like putting in a sink or a toilet, but it wasn't easy. Maybe once he'd received his prosthesis things would be different. He had an appointment to return to the rehab doc at the Battle Creek VA in a couple of days. He hoped the prosthesis would be ready by then.

He crossed over to where his younger sister waited. "How do you want to get this done? And why are we listening to this crap? What's wrong with good old-fashioned rock and roll?"

"Finally, a reason to shut this stuff off," Jazz said, crossing over to the radio. She played with the dials until she found something he recognized. "Is this better?"

"Much."

"I heard that," Dalton called from the bathroom. "This counts against you, Jazz."

"No, it doesn't. I still get my two hours," she tossed back. She was smiling, so he understood this was an ongoing joke between them. "Ready? I'm going to lift the drywall into place, and you're going to help drive the screws in." As she spoke, Jazz reached down to pull up one end of a large sheet of drywall.

He propped one crutch up against the wall, then used his free arm to help her lift. The sucker was heavy, and he couldn't help being impressed by Jazz's strength. A thin layer of white drywall dust covered her dark hair that was pulled away from her face in a ponytail.

The twins were close but complete opposites. Jemma was girlie and learned to cook from their grandmother while Jazz was the tomboy who had preferred following their grandfather around, helping him do home repair work. Together, they made the perfect team to run a B&B.

Sweat beaded on his brow, but he ignored it as he helped wrestle the Sheetrock into place. Jazz held it with two hands, leaving him to screw it in place with the power drill.

It was slow and awkward, but they managed to secure that sheet before moving on to the next. After the first two, they found a decent rhythm as they worked their way down the long living room wall.

"Hey! Dinner will be ready in ninety minutes," Jemma's voice carried loudly up the stairs. "That gives you an hour to work and thirty minutes to clean up."

"Got it," Jazz called.

Jonas paused and swiped his face with the hem of his T-shirt. "Think we can finish it by then?"

"Hope so." Jazz bent over and pulled a saw over. "Take a quick break, I need to cut this last piece to make it fit."

Something else he couldn't do. Swallowing his ire, he rested against the wall, not willing to admit how much this small bit of physical labor had taken out of him. Yeah, he'd only just gotten out of the hospital today, but the last few weeks had been spent on a rehab unit, in which he'd done therapy for at least four hours a day.

Construction work was very different from the exercises his therapists had thrown at him.

Jazz measured, then set up the drywall along the saw. The blade whined loudly as it cut through the Sheetrock, throwing more dust into her face and hair. She wore goggles over her eyes, and he was impressed at how easily she accomplished the task.

Nothing like being shown up by your kid sister, he thought sourly.

"Okay, ready?" Jazz lifted the newly shaved section of drywall, and he pushed away from the wall, bending over to lend a hand.

When they had the board in place, he pulled up the drill and began anchoring the screws to keep it in place. He worked his way all along the top edges, then handed the drill to Jazz so she could do the lower section.

He shifted out of the way but misjudged the distance. Or maybe he was just tired, because he caught the edge of the saw with his crutch. Knocked off balance, he tried to keep himself upright but couldn't.

To his horror, he fell down hard, catching the edge of the saw blade. Pain lanced his side, but the burn of humiliation was much, much worse.

"Jonas! Are you okay?"

"Leave me alone." His tone was sharper than he intended, but he managed to push himself upright, bracing himself on his knees. The lower part of his left leg throbbed worse than his side from where he landed on the saw. Mortified, he glanced up at his sister. "Hand me my crutches."

Jazz looked as if she might cry as she scrambled to grab them. When he had them both, he braced his weight on his left knee, ignoring the pain, and managed to get his right foot beneath him. It wasn't pretty, but he finally levered himself upright.

"Jonas, you're hurt." Jazz reached out a hand, but he instinctively shunned away.

"I'm fine." He wanted nothing more than to get out of there, to hide in a corner to lick his wounds. It's exactly what had happened the day the bomb went off, and he abruptly realized his wounded animal instincts were here to stay.

"Jonas, wait." Jazz hurried after him, but he didn't stop. "You're bleeding!"

He didn't care about the wound in his side, his left leg hurt far worse.

The sooner he was out of there, the better.

~

Bella parked her car in front of The McNallys' B&B and slid out from behind the wheel. She felt refreshed after spending the past two hours exploring the town. Being on the lake was wonderful, the gently lapping waves against the rocky shore soothed away her annoyance with the crabby Jonas.

As she dug in her purse for her key, the guy she'd tried to pry out of her mind came hobbling out from the garage. His face was pulled into a grimace, his skin red and smeared with a mixture of sweat and dirt. She paused, sensing his distress.

"What happened?" She moved toward him, noticing the blood staining the left side of his torso.

"Nothing." His curt tone did not invite conversation. He continued his path toward the house.

She suppressed a sigh. Why was it that men had to be so difficult? "Jemma will be mad if you leave a trail of blood through your grandparents' great room."

That made him pause. Bella found it interesting that he cared about his sister's reaction more so than his own injury.

"Let me take a look." She approached cautiously, half expecting him to bolt. "I'm sure I can patch you up enough that you won't bleed all over the place."

He dropped his head as if unable to stand looking at her. She wondered if he had a personal issue with her, or just with nurses in general? She suspected he'd recently been released from a rehab facility and took note that he wasn't using a prosthesis yet.

"Do you have a first aid kit?" The words were forced through his clenched teeth.

"Do I have a first aid kit?" She scoffed at his foolishness. "What self-respecting nurse doesn't have a first aid kit? Mine is so big it doesn't fit in my glove box."

She thought the corner of his mouth quirked again, but it could have been her imagination. Whatever. He was a tough nut to crack.

And why she was tempted to waste time cracking that outer shell of his, she had no clue. He wasn't the first injured vet she'd cared for and wouldn't be the last.

Well, maybe he was the last, depending on what happened with the hospital's investigation into the medication error.

She went to her car, unlatched the trunk, and found the twelve-by-twelve-inch plastic box that she used to carry her first aid supplies. She opened it up and rummaged through the items to find what she needed. "Why don't you come over here to sit on the bumper?"

Jonas hesitated for so long she thought he'd changed his mind, but he eventually made his way to her car. He sat on the edge of the trunk, then put both crutches off to one side. "I'm fine. Just slap a dressing over it so I don't track blood inside."

It was the longest sentence he'd uttered, and she was touched by the fact that he cared about his sister's feelings. A tough nut with a gooey nugget buried inside.

"Depends on how bad it is." Up close, heat emanated from his skin, and the mixture of dust and sweat was far more appealing than it should be. The flash of attraction was annoying and unwelcome. She was only here for ten days. Once she knew what her future held, she'd either head back to her job in Battle Creek or move on to some other place.

When he lifted the edge of his T-shirt, she was surprised to find two puncture wounds still oozing blood amidst the scrapes and bruising. "What, did you fall on a couple of ice picks?"

Again with the slight quirk of his mouth. "Saw blade."

"I hope your tetanus shots are up to date." Since he'd been in the Army and had been hospitalized recently, she had to assume they were. Bella moistened a gauze with a small bottle of saline and began cleaning the wound. Jonas never flinched, but she sensed he was in pain. "Did you hurt anything else on the way down? Have any other injuries I need to look at?"

"No. I'm fine."

Sure he was. She mentally rolled her eyes. Heaven forbid he actually be honest with her. She didn't glance down at his injured left leg but logically deduced since he'd fallen on his left side, the leg must have gotten banged around. The skin covering an amputation site was fragile and tender—to the point that patients often felt as if the missing part of the limb was still there. The doctors described it as phantom pain. In this instance, if he'd injured the freshly healed wound, it likely hurt like a son of a gun.

She wanted to ask if he was planning to use a prosthetic device but knew he didn't particularly like talking about his injury.

He'd rather use it as a shield to prevent anyone from getting close.

When the area was cleaned up, she could see the two

puncture sites weren't as deep as she'd originally thought. Which was a good thing. Doing her best to ignore Jonas's rock-hard abs and lean muscular build, she put a small pressure dressing over the sites and then applied a thick white adhesive bandage over it to keep it in place.

Jonas glanced down at her handiwork. "I told you to slap something over it. That dressing won't survive a shower."

"Lucky for you, I have more supplies." She closed the lid of the box with a snap. "I can reapply a fresh dressing when you've finished with your shower."

"I can do it." He still didn't meet her gaze. "No reason to bother you."

He bothered her just by being contrary, but she didn't tell him that. What was it about Jonas that tempted her to push his buttons?

"Yeah, because slapping a dressing over a wound is a real bother." She picked up the first aid kit and thrust it at him. "Give it back to me when you're finished."

He grabbed the box, then glanced at his crutches. No way could he carry the first aid kit while using the crutches. She sighed and tugged it back. "I'll carry it."

His jaw flexed, and she sensed he wanted to snap at her again.

"Go ahead," she taunted. "Tell me what's going on in your mind. I work with arrogant surgeons all day. I can take it."

Jonas's brown gaze clashed with hers, and she could see the spark of anger shimmering there. Without another word, he reached for the crutches and stood on his good leg. She tucked the first aid kit under her arm and followed him inside the B&B.

They barely made it inside the great room when Jemma

rushed forward, her brow furrowed with concern. "Jonas! Are you okay?"

"I patched him up, nothing to worry about." Again, she wasn't sure why she was inserting herself into the McNally family drama.

Jonas glanced at her—was that a speck of gratitude she saw there?—Before making his way toward the staircase. He didn't respond to his sister, navigating the stairs easily. No doubt, his pride was hurt more than anything else.

"Thanks, Bella," Jemma whispered once Jonas disappeared inside his room. "I heard he took a bad fall."

"Yeah, but trust me, he's fine." Bella turned to face Jemma. "Word of advice?" When the woman nodded, she went on, "The more you fuss over him, the harder he'll try to push you away."

Jemma winced. "I know. But it's difficult not to hover when someone you love is going through a difficult time."

Bella nodded. "I get it, but I think he's on the brink of bolting already. I've taken care of wounded soldiers before, so I recognize the signs. Just trust me on this, okay?"

Jemma's troubled gaze was focused on the top of the staircase. "He never bothered to tell us about the injury. Just showed up with his foot missing. It kills me to know how long he must have suffered in the hospital without any of us being there for him."

Bella didn't have a response to that. If Jonas wouldn't confide in his family, she wasn't sure who he'd confide in. Finally, she said, "He doesn't want sympathy. He wants to find a way to get back to normal. Or whatever his new normal is."

"You're right." Jemma tipped her head to the side, regarding her thoughtfully. "Bella, would you mind joining us for dinner?"

"Um, dinner?" She was fairly certain she'd read on The McNallys' B&B website that breakfast was the only meal that was provided along with the room.

"Yes, dinner." Jemma smiled. "You won't be disappointed. I'm a decent cook."

Bella hesitated, certain there was an ulterior motive for Jemma's spontaneous invitation.

If she were smart, she'd decline and leave the McNallys to themselves. The last thing she wanted to do was spend more time with the surly, silent, and stubborn Jonas.

"I'd like that, thanks." The words popped out of her mouth before she could call them back.

Inwardly railing at herself for being a fool, Bella carried the first aid kit up the grand staircase. Instead of leaving it outside the door of Jonas's room, she took it to hers. If he wanted it, he'd have to come ask for it.

Yep, she was a glutton for punishment all right. Somehow, despite all the warning signs, Bella was looking forward to the next verbal tussle with Jonas McNally.

CHAPTER THREE

Jonas felt better after a hot shower. Sure, the entire left side of his body still ached, especially his lower leg, but he figured he may as well get used to it. The situation wasn't going to change any time soon.

This was his new reality.

The puncture wounds were bleeding again, so he stuffed a wad of tissue over them and tried to hold it in place with his elbow. When that didn't work, he used some of the tape from the old dressing to keep it in place. With a towel cinched around his waist, he crutched to the doorway and opened it a crack to see if Bella had left the first aid kit for him.

She hadn't. Despite his annoyance, he felt the corner of his mouth twitch with amusement. Bella was a feisty one and had no doubt taken the kit to her room on purpose. Just to piss him off.

For some odd reason, he liked that about her.

Her smart mouth probably drove the surgeons crazy. The image abruptly made him frown. Yeah, he needed to remember that while he might enjoy sparring with her, there could be nothing more serious between them. Bella was beautiful and funny, but she was a nurse who worked with doctors all day long. No reason she'd be interested in a deformed former special ops soldier with an uncertain future.

Rhonda, his girlfriend, had taken one look at him in the hospital and had left in a hurry. So much for sticking around through sickness and in health.

Or a missing foot.

Right. So that's that. He grimaced as he rifled through his duffel, searching for clean clothes. He wanted to pull on a pair of shorts in deference to the June summer heat, but that would leave his amputated limb hanging out for anyone to see. Instead, he opted for a set of army green cargo pants. The long pants leg would hide his injury. He couldn't bear the thought of people staring at what was left of his lower leg. Shirtless, the makeshift dressing hanging precariously from a bit of tape stuck to the left side of his chest, he made his way out of the room to knock on Bella's door.

"Shocker," she said in lieu of a greeting. Her gaze lingered a moment too long on his bare chest, and he felt his body tighten with awareness. "Macho man that you are, I would have bet money you would decide against borrowing my first aid kit."

"And you'd have lost," he countered. "No blood in Jemma's house, remember?"

"That's right. You do have a heart, at least where your sister is concerned." Bella turned and crossed over to the bed. The first aid kit was already open. She peeled apart a new dressing and glanced back, frowning when she noted he was still hovering in the doorway. "What? Are you afraid I'll try to ravage you if you cross the threshold?"

Frankly, he was more concerned about what she'd goad him into doing, like kissing her senseless, but of course he didn't say that. Shaking his head at his foolishness, he crutched into the room. "I can put the dressing on myself."

"Easier for me to do it." She pulled off his field dressing and peered at the injury. "Not bad. I'll put antibiotic ointment on those wounds, too." As she spoke, she used a dab of the ointment, then smoothed a fresh layer of gauze over the wounds.

He didn't say anything, wishing she'd hurry as he liked the feel of her hands on his skin far too much. This close he was hyperaware of her strawberry scent, and he wondered why on earth his senses had come alive for this woman.

Wrong place, wrong time. Wrong everything.

"That looks good." She dropped the roll of adhesive tape into the kit and stepped back. "I'll pick up some waterproof dressings after dinner, if you'd like."

"No need." His voice was low and gruff, and he avoided her gaze. He used the crutches to move away from her, heading toward the door. "I can get my own supplies."

"Yes, I'm sure you can." Her dry tone was laced with sarcasm. "Okay, I'll see you later, then. Sounds as if your sister will have dinner ready soon."

Her words stopped him at the door, and he craned his neck around to stare at her. "Since when are B and B guests invited to dinner?"

"Since your sister seems to think she has to thank me for providing first aid to you." Bella's smile didn't reach her eyes. "Besides, if her cooking is half as good as her baking, why wouldn't I jump at the chance of a free home-cooked meal? Especially since I'm hungry."

Jonas glared at her, knowing full well the real reason Jemma had invited her to dine with them was because she was attempting to play matchmaker. A futile and ridiculous effort on his behalf.

The better question was why Bella had agreed to Jemma's rather transparent ploy? Especially when she didn't look particularly happy about it?

Not for a free meal, that was for sure.

He wasn't quick enough to come up with a response, so he hobbled back down the hall to his room. He pulled a clean white T-shirt over his head, then lowered himself to the edge of the bed.

He hadn't even been there for twenty-four hours and he already seriously regretted his decision to stay here while he finished recuperating. Obviously, he hadn't thought things through. Now that he was here, he couldn't tolerate the idea of Jemma and Jazz worrying about him, and he'd already made a fool of himself in front of his future brother-in-law while attempting to prove himself useful.

For a long moment he seriously considered heading downstairs, getting into his car, and driving away. Jazz's wedding wasn't until the following weekend, he could always come back for the ceremony.

"Jonas? You coming?" Jemma's voice drifted up to his room, and he heard the hint of concern in her tone.

"Yeah." Swallowing a groan, he pushed himself upward and grabbed the despised crutches. After using them for the past seven weeks, he was forced to acknowledge that having a prosthetic device would be better than this.

After navigating the stairs, he found his way to the kitchen. Something smelled delicious, and the first pang of hunger in weeks stirred in his belly.

"Chicken pot pie?" Was it possible his sister had made his favorite just for him?

Jemma blushed and nodded. "Used Grandma's recipe

and spent all afternoon making them. Thank goodness for central air or I never would have survived. Tomorrow we'll have to grill out, the temperature is supposed to hit ninety degrees."

Everyone was seated at the large kitchen table, including a dark-haired stranger dressed in a brown sheriff's deputy uniform. The way he cut up food for Trey, Jemma's son and his three-year-old nephew, Jonas assumed he was Jemma's fiancé.

"Garth Lewis." The stranger paused in his task long enough to stand and offer his hand.

"Jonas McNally." It was interesting Jemma had gotten herself engaged to a cop, despite her divorce from another cop. Rumor had it her ex had serious control issues and a hot temper. Jonas thought the ex was lucky Jonas had been deployed overseas or he would have had to rearrange his face. He focused his attention on Garth. "I understand congratulations are in order. Seems both twins have gotten themselves engaged in the past couple of months."

"Thank you. I—we couldn't be happier." Garth shared a secret smile with Jemma that caused Jonas to look away. The love shimmering between them was too painful to watch.

The only vacant spot at the long picnic-style table was between the wall and Bella, no doubt manipulated by one of the twins. Swallowing a curse, he propped the crutches on the wall and lowered himself into the empty space.

Bella subtly leaned away from him, her gaze centered on Jazz and Dalton. "I'm so impressed by the work you're doing on the apartment over the garage."

"That's nothing." Jemma set an individually baked pot pie in front of each person, including him. His mouth watered with anticipation. "You should see the work they're doing on the old Stevenson place. Dalton bought the house back in April and then used his architect skills to redesign the main level. They're basically starting over from scratch, but it's going to be amazing when it's finished."

"I'd love a tour when you have time." Bella finally glanced at him. "Have you seen it, Jonas?"

"Not yet." He was preoccupied with the meal in front of him. Using his fork, he poked a small hole in the top of the golden brown crust, releasing the tantalizing scent of baked chicken and veggies. "Jemma, this smells amazing."

"I hope you like it." His sister brought the last two pies to the table for her and Garth.

"How could I not?" He took a bite and almost moaned out loud. The flaky crust and the chicken sauce smothering the tender chicken and veggies tasted exactly like his grandmother's. A sense of loss hit hard. He wished he'd been able to return home for his grandmother's funeral, but he'd been deep in the mountains of Afghanistan, and by the time he'd learned about her passing, the funeral had already been over.

"I can't believe you made these from scratch." Bella's voice echoed with amazement. "The only chicken pot pies I've had were out of the freezer at the grocery store."

"Those are disgusting." Jazz wrinkled her nose.

"Well, they weren't until now," Bella argued. "Obviously once you've tasted the real thing, there's no going back."

"You have that right." Jonas spoke without thinking. "Nothing beats Grandma's recipe."

"Can't argue, it's delicious." Bella's arm lightly brushed against his, and he forced himself not to pull away from the heat of her skin.

"Bella, tell us about yourself," Jazz invited.

"Oh, there's nothing much to tell." Bella waved her fork

in a casual gesture, but Jonas noticed she went tense. "I'm just taking a badly needed break from work, that's all."

"Where do you work?" Jemma persisted.

There was a moment's hesitation before she answered. "At the VA hospital in Battle Creek. I'm a nurse in the operating room."

It was a small world. Too small. Jonas steered the conversation away from Bella, back to his siblings. "Jazz, do you have everything you need for the wedding?"

"Everything except finalizing the music." She playfully elbowed Dalton in the ribs. "Not surprising we can't seem to agree on some of the songs."

"Hey." Dalton rubbed his side as if injured. "It's not my fault you have awful taste in music."

"Me? You're the one who likes that country stuff. I'm not walking down the aisle to 'Mammas Don't Let Your Babies Grow Up to be Cowboys.'" Jazz added a nasal twang as she sang the title of the song that almost made him laugh.

"If you ask me, you both have terrible taste in music." Once again, he spoke without thinking, and all the faces turned to look at him in surprise. He lifted a brow and spread his hands wide. "Are you kidding me? Rock and roll is here to stay. End of discussion."

"I have to agree with Dalton on this one," Garth spoke up. "Country rules."

"No way. It's Jazz's big day, she should get to decide the music." Jemma was a staunch supporter of her twin.

It occurred to Jonas that it had been a long time, over eighteen months, since he'd been stateside. And he'd missed the family banter that accompanied their occasional family meals.

"What kind of music does Jazz like?" Bella asked.

"Eighties tunes," Garth and Dalton answered at the same time.

"Why she likes that particular decade of music when she wasn't even born yet is beyond me," Dalton added.

"I have to agree with Jonas on the rock and roll," Bella announced. "You're all a bunch of crazy people."

"I'm not crazy," Trey protested.

That cracked up several of the adults, and even Jonas managed to smile. He looked down at his plate, surprised to see he'd eaten every bite of Jemma's chicken pot pie. Her cooking had succeeded in whetting his appetite when all else had failed.

"You have a nice smile, Jonas." Bella sent him a sly wink. "You should let it out more often."

He felt the tips of his ears burning with embarrassment that she'd noticed but couldn't think of a snappy comeback, so let it go.

He thought about his half-baked plan to get out of Dodge after everyone was asleep. Sharing dinner together had changed his mind.

It was good to be home.

The smile transformed Jonas's face in a way that made her heart thump erratically in her chest. If he was handsome before, Jonas was stunningly attractive when he grinned.

Wow. It was a good thing he wasn't smiling all the time, otherwise there would be a trail of broken hearts scattered across the country.

But not hers. Bella found herself thinking about her fiancé, Greg Wallace, and her brother, Ryan. Both men had died while serving their country, leaving her with two folded flags, a handful of love letters, and her memories.

She wasn't interested in men. They were either slime-buckets or had more baggage than she was interested in carting around.

Losing her brother and her fiancé was more than enough.

After setting her fork down, she nudged her plate away, her appetite having vanished. She caught Jonas's gaze eyeing her plate and pushed it toward him. "Finish it off," she encouraged. "I'm full."

He cast her a glance that called her bluff but didn't hesitate to clean her plate.

"Anyone save room for rhubarb pie?" Jemma asked.

Bella could have sworn she heard Jonas groan. "You baked another of my favorites?"

Suddenly, she needed to get away. "None for me, thanks." Bella carried her empty plate to the counter. "Do you want me to start washing dishes?"

"No! You're our guest!" Jemma's expression of horror was comical.

"A guest who was welcomed into the family meal," Bella pointed out. Through the kitchen window she could see the rippling blue lake water beckoning her.

"I don't need help cleaning up," Jemma said firmly. "Are you sure you won't try the pie?"

"I'm sure." She could feel Jonas's gaze boring into her but refused to look at him. The desire to get away couldn't be ignored. "If you'll excuse me?" She made a hasty retreat from the kitchen, heading toward the whitewashed gazebo overlooking the lakeshore.

Hearing the sloshing of the waves helped ease the tension.

It wasn't like her to wallow over events in the past, to commiserate over things she couldn't change. As a nurse, she'd seen more than her fair share of illness and death, something that helped her to focus on the positive aspects of life.

Being physically healthy and able to work was a blessing. One she didn't take for granted. If she was fired from her job at the Battle Creek VA, she'd find something else.

There was always a shortage of nurses. And maybe this time she'd try something other than surgery. She wasn't feeling kindly toward surgeons these days.

Jemma had plastic chairs in the gazebo, so she took a seat and stared at the water. There were plenty of people in their boats, enjoying the beautiful summer weather. The breeze off the lake was nice.

Maybe she should become a traveling nurse. She and Ryan had lost their parents a few years ago, so it wasn't as if she had any family holding her here in Michigan. Normally she liked the friendly people of the Midwest, but living near water, either a lake or the ocean, held a definite appeal.

She sat watching the boats on the water for what seemed like forever but was likely only an hour when she heard something behind her. A glance over her shoulder confirmed her suspicions.

Jonas.

"What's wrong?" His blunt question surprised her. She'd expected him to avoid treading on personal ground.

"Why do you think something is wrong?"

"Why are you answering a question with another question?"

Touché. She had to smile. "Nothing, really. Your family is really nice."

"They are." He clumped over and dropped into the seat beside her. "And you miss your brother."

Her eyes burned with tears. "Yes. Both of your brothers-in-law-to-be remind me of him. They give as good as they get."

"He was older, wasn't he?"

"Good guess." She shrugged. "Three years. I almost followed him into the Army. Figured I'd be an amazing Army nurse."

"Why didn't you?"

She slanted him a sideways look. "I don't take orders very well."

"No, really?" His dry humor made her smile. "I hadn't noticed."

"When I spoke with Ryan over Skype, I could see that being out there was more difficult than he'd anticipated." She paused, then added, "I'm sure you felt the same way."

He nodded but didn't say anything more.

For a full five minutes they simply watched the lake. "What happened at Battle Creek?"

His keen perception caught her off guard. "What do you mean?"

"Bella." He sighed. "No one comes out to McNally Bay for ten days without a good reason. It's not that much of a tourist attraction. Obviously, you're hiding from something."

"Like you are?" The instant she said the words she wished she could take them back. She lifted a hand. "I'm sorry, that was rude. You're not hiding out here, you came to see your family and to attend your sister's wedding."

Jonas nodded. "I was thinking of bolting out of here, but Jemma's cooking is too good to pass up." He lightly bumped her shoulder. "The company isn't too bad either."

Was that a compliment? "Wow, color me surprised."

He turned in his seat to look her directly in the eye. "Actually, I'd like to paint you instead."

"Huh? Excuse me? Did you say paint?"

Jonas flexed his hands open and closed, watching his fingers work as if seeing them for the first time. "I used to dabble in drawing and painting, but living as a starving artist didn't appeal. Obviously, my stint in the Army didn't work out either, so I thought it might be good to get back to my art. I'll need to drive into town to pick up supplies, so we can't start until tomorrow."

Her jaw dropped, not just by his request, which was a doozy, but because he'd actually strung a series of sentences together to make a full paragraph. "Uh, sure. I guess. I'm not sure I'm good artist material or that I can sit still for long periods of time, but happy to help."

"Thanks."

Jonas an artist? She hadn't seen that one coming. They remained sitting in the gazebo, watching the waves when she heard a deep voice from behind her.

"Izabella? I need to talk to you."

The familiar drawl of Dr. Eli Hackbarth made the hairs on the back of her neck rise in alarm. It took every ounce of willpower not to jump up and scream at him. Instead, she took her time, shifting in her seat so that she could look at him.

The surgeon looked ridiculous standing in the hot June sun wearing his Armani suit.

"I'm sorry." Ice dripped from her tone. "My lawyer has instructed me not to talk to anyone about the case."

"Your lawyer?" Hackbarth looked shocked. "You have a lawyer?"

"Why not? You have one." She sensed Jonas standing beside her and turned to face him. "Let's go inside, okay?"

"Sure thing." Jonas drilled Hackbarth with a steely glare

as he followed her back inside the B&B. Once they were inside, she let her breath out in a heavy sigh.

"We need to talk," Jonas said in a low tone.

"Not really. I'm fine." She walked past him to head up to her room. She was relieved Jonas let her, despite knowing she was far from all right. She wasn't in the mood to tell him her dark secret. She was more concerned with what had just happened.

How had Eli Hackbarth found her at The McNallys' B&B?

And what exactly did he want from her?

CHAPTER FOUR

Jonas watched Bella disappear up the stairs, then headed outside intending to confront the guy, a surgeon no doubt, who'd shown up looking for her.

But by the time he'd made his way out to the front of the house, he only caught a brief glimpse of the back of a sports car driving away. To his eye, it appeared to be a black Porsche.

Fit perfectly with his stuck-up image of the guy who'd shown up wearing some ridiculously overpriced suit.

Hearing how both the assumed surgeon and Bella had lawyers was disturbing. Something bad had happened at the Battle Creek VA, and he wanted to know the details.

He turned and headed inside, meeting Jemma in the great room. "Something wrong?"

"Maybe." He frowned, deciding she needed to know the truth. "Sounds like some sort of legal issue between some surgeon and Bella. He came here to talk, but she sent him on his way."

"Legal issue?" Jemma's eyes widened in surprise. "That doesn't sound good."

No, it didn't. But it wasn't their mess to worry about. Unless the B&B was somehow involved.

"I'm sure she'll be okay." He made a mental note to grill Bella for information in the morning before turning his attention to his sister. "Listen, Jemma, give up on the matchmaking, will you?"

"Matchmaking?" Her eyes widened with feigned surprise. "I don't know what you're talking about."

"Yes, you do. And while I appreciate that you and Jazz have both found love, there's no reason to push the rest of us in that direction. Especially me. I have enough going on in my life right now, understand? Besides, Bella isn't interested. No sense in losing a guest over this."

"I'm not matchmaking," Jemma insisted, although her gaze skittered from his. "I only invited Bella to dinner to make her feel welcome here, and to repay her kindness in helping you out."

"Yeah, right." He didn't hide his sarcasm. "Just knock it off, okay? Good night."

"Good night. Oh, and Jonas?"

He paused, glancing at her over his shoulder. "What?"

"Dalton and Jazz could really use your help tomorrow with the loft apartment. If you're feeling up to it."

He was surprised to hear they wanted him back after his debacle of a fall. Then again, he could tell Jemma was looking forward to having a bedroom for Trey.

"Yeah, I'll do my best." Not to fall flat on my face, he silently added.

"That would be great, thank you, Jonas." Gratitude shimmered in her tone.

He could feel her anxious gaze on his back as he made his way upstairs. Crutching up was exhausting, and twice he teetered backward, catching himself before he tumbled down on his butt. Man, he had to find a way to get his full strength back, that was for sure.

After popping a couple of ibuprofen, he absolutely refused to take narcotics, Jonas crawled into bed.

Nights were the worst. In the darkness, the images of what he'd experienced when his team had walked into a minefield of hidden bombs haunted him incessantly. He closed his eyes and pictured Bella and the lake in his mind in an effort to ward them off.

When he awoke to the morning sun, he stared at the alarm clock on the bedside table in surprise. He'd slept through the entire night? He swung his legs over the edge of the bed and ran his fingers through his shaggy hair, trying to figure out why he'd slept so well. Because he was home with family or because he'd physically exhausted himself helping with the construction project?

Likely a combination of both.

His stomach rumbled with hunger, his appetite having returned full force, so he quickly dressed and headed downstairs to breakfast. The dining room was empty except for Bella, so he dropped into the seat across from her.

"Good morning." He offered a lopsided smile. "You okay?"

"Of course!" Bella's smile was forced. "Good morning to you, too. How's your injury?"

"Fine." He wanted to say more, but Jemma came out of the kitchen carrying a coffeepot.

"Jonas, what would you like for breakfast? I'm offering the full Irish or eggs Benedict."

"The full Irish." He knew Jemma learned to make his grandmother's signature breakfast and couldn't wait to taste it again after eating hospital food and rations overseas. Maybe his loss of appetite wasn't related to being depressed the way the doctor had told him but because he hadn't been offered any decent food. Until now.

"Two full Irish breakfasts coming right up." Jemma refilled Bella's coffee, then headed back into the kitchen.

"Do you need more dressings?" Bella asked.

"Why don't you take a break from playing nurse for the rest of the day?" The suggestion came out sharper than he intended, so he tried to soften it up by adding, "You're on vacation, remember?"

Bella shrugged and peered into her mug of coffee as if seeking answers in the dark depths. "I'm heading into town after breakfast, I can give you a ride in if you'd like."

He wanted nothing more than to get his painting supplies, but he had promised to help in the garage apartment. "I need to help Jazz and Dalton, so I won't have time until later."

"Maybe I can help, too?"

He frowned, trying to understand. "You mean help do construction work?"

"Why not?" She met his gaze head-on. "I'm sure there's something I can do."

"Blueberry muffins and lemon-poppy seed bread," Jemma announced, setting a plate on their table. "Your breakfast will be out shortly."

"Yum." Bella took a slice of the bread. "Jemma, I'm going to need to take up running if I stay here too long."

Jonas tried not to dwell on the fact that running wasn't a part of his future. Yeah, he'd seen pictures of men running with a prosthesis, but he needed to learn to walk first. He helped himself to a blueberry muffin and had to admit it was delicious.

Why had Bella offered to help them work on the apartment? For something to do? Had she realized that spending time in a small town wasn't as fun as she'd thought?

Soon they were both too busy devouring Jemma's breakfast to talk further. The full Irish tasted exactly the way his grandmother's used to, and he had to give Jemma the credit she was due. The McNallys' B&B will clearly be a huge success based on the food alone.

"That was amazing," Bella said as she sat back in her chair. "I'm not kidding. I'll really need to take up running if I'm going to stay here every day."

"Do you like running?"

She wrinkled her nose. "Not really. But I need to do something to stay in shape."

"There are bikes for rent in town," he offered. Maybe once he had his prosthesis he'd be able to ride a bicycle. "Might be one way to explore."

She eyed him over the rim of her mug. "Is that your way of getting rid of me? I get the sense you don't want my help on the garage apartment."

He realized she was more perceptive than he gave her credit for. "Hey, you can do what you want. It's your vacation."

Jemma came out of the kitchen and smiled when she picked up their empty plates. "Would you like anything else?"

"Not me, but it was absolutely delicious." Bella's praise caused his sister's cheeks to go pink with pride.

"I agree," he added. "That was the best breakfast I've had in two months."

Jemma's smile faded. "Two months? You were in the hospital for two months and you didn't call us until two weeks ago?"

He mentally kicked himself for bringing up his hospitalization. He reached for his crutches and quickly left the dining area without responding to his sister's accusation.

There was nothing he could say in his defense. And talking about those dark days after his injury wouldn't help.

All he could do was move forward. Learn to accept his physical limitations while finding a way to live as a civilian.

Easier said than done.

～

Bella wasn't sure why she'd offered to work on the garage apartment when she'd never worked on a construction project before in her life. In fact, she wasn't even sure she liked doing construction work. Did she even know how to drive a nail into a board without injuring herself?

Not likely.

But now that she'd opened her big mouth, she was determined to see it through.

If she were honest with herself, she'd admit that seeing Eli Hackbarth last evening had rattled her and that she didn't relish the thought of being alone. Crazy? Maybe. It wasn't as if she lived in fear of the arrogant surgeon.

But she didn't like the way he'd found her at the B&B either. She'd only told her friend Chrissy about her plans, and Chrissy didn't much like Hackbarth either. So why would her friend rat her out?

She had no idea.

Bella sat at the dining room table for a long five minutes after Jonas had stalked off. Again, she wasn't in the mood to deal with family drama, and it seemed that the McNallys had their fair share of problems.

Easier to deal with theirs than to think about her own bleak future.

No family. No fiancé. No job. Ugh!

Enough wallowing in self-pity. She drained her coffee mug and headed up to her room to use the bathroom and to dress in a pair of old cut-off jean shorts and a ratty T-shirt. She pulled on a pair of running shoes, idly considering going for a quick run, then rejecting the idea. Eli Hackbarth had likely already returned to Battle Creek, but she didn't want to risk running into him on the off chance he'd stuck around.

Implying she had a lawyer had been a bit of an exaggeration. She'd talked to a lawyer friend who'd given her advice, but she hadn't hired him to take her case.

But Hackbarth didn't need to know that.

Following the sounds of hammering and upbeat eighties tunes, she made her way to the second story apartment in the garage. Jazz and Jonas were putting up drywall in the kitchen area while Dalton was working in the bathroom nestled between the two bedrooms.

Lifting her voice above the eighties music, she tried to get Dalton's attention. "What can I do to help?"

He looked up at her. "Hey, Bella, are you sure about this? We've never put our guests to work."

"I bet you don't invite guests for dinner either, but you did." She waved a dismissive hand. "I'm here, what do you need?"

"If you're willing to sand these drywall seams, I can work on finishing up the mudding in the bedrooms. Soon the walls will be ready for paint."

She eyed the wall and the sander in his hand. How hard could it be? "I can do that."

"Great." He handed her the belt sander and a pair of safety goggles, then showed her how to use the sander.

The eighties music wasn't easy to hear over the vibration

of the sander, but she found herself humming along to the melody anyway.

Sanding the seams wasn't difficult but was time-consuming. She was covered in white dust five minutes into her task. Her thoughts bounced between why Eli Hackbarth had wanted to talk to her and to Jonas and how he was faring with the task of hanging drywall.

After finishing one wall, her arms ached from lifting the sander and moving it down the drywall seams. Talk about being out of shape! She set it down and bent at the waist, dangling her arms at her sides. After a few minutes, she went back to work on the next wall. Thankfully, there were only three walls to do as the doorway took up most of the space. By the time she finished the second wall, her biceps were screaming in protest. Once again she bent over and dangled her arms, thinking about how she didn't exactly love construction work.

"Are you okay?"

Jonas's voice caught her off guard, and she straightened so quickly the room spun for a moment. "Fine!" He stood in the doorway with his crutches, his dark gaze intense. "Why? Did I miss something?"

He didn't speak for a long moment, his eyes searching hers. She resisted the urge to wipe the dust away, knowing it was useless. Besides, he was covered in dust, too.

"We've finished with the drywall. Come check it out."

She followed him into the open-concept living space. "Looks great. What's next?"

"More taping and mudding of the drywall seams." Jazz crossed over to stand next to them. "Once we have that done, we can paint."

"When do you anticipate finishing this up?" Bella could tell it was coming along, but it also looked as if they had a long way to go. Especially since all she'd done to contribute was sand drywall seams on the bathroom walls.

"Hopefully in a few weeks." Jazz shrugged, raking her gaze over the area. "Three at the most."

"Impressive. I bet Jemma can't wait to move in." She forced herself to turn back toward the bathroom. "I have another wall to finish."

"Take a break." There was a note of steel beneath Jonas's tone. "I'll do the last wall in the bathroom. When that's finished, we can head into town."

A glance at her watch confirmed they'd only been working for two hours. "Are you sure?"

"Trust me, we appreciate what you've done already," Jazz said. "Thanks to you and Jonas we're ahead of schedule. I'm a taping queen, but Dalton is better at mudding. After the bathroom is finished, there's nothing more you can do until it's time to paint. I mean"—she looked flustered—"if you're interested in painting, that is. If not, that's okay, too."

"I can help paint," Jonas said. "Bella is here to relax."

"I don't mind painting." She didn't love it, but she didn't mind it. "But I think for now I'll take a shower."

"I'll catch up with you in a little while." Jonas crutched to the bathroom. She watched for a moment as he set the crutches against the wall, then carefully bent down to pick up the sander. Bracing his left hand on the wall, he went to work, the muscles in his arms flexing as he moved the sander over the bumpy seam.

Tearing her gaze from him wasn't easy. Calling herself every kind of a fool, she turned and headed down the stairs. The sunshine was blinding, and she shaded her hand over her eyes as she looked around the small parking lot.

There was no sign of Hackbarth. Just her car, Jonas's car, and the cherry red truck that she knew belonged to Jazz.

No other guests at the B&B at the moment, although according to Jemma there were several bookings that were due to arrive tomorrow, which was Friday, and staying through the weekend.

She brushed off as much dust as she could before walking inside the house and up to her room. Oddly enough, she was looking forward to going into town with Jonas. Had he been teasing about wanting to paint her? Did she even want to sit there while he studied her?

Goose bumps rippled along her arms, and she told herself to stop thinking about this upcoming trip as anything but two lonely people sharing a ride into town. She'd planned to visit the quilt shop while he went to find his art supplies.

They were carpooling, nothing more.

When she finished showering the dust off, she donned a pair of white capri pants and a light blue tank top. Sliding her feet into a pair of light blue flip-flops, she was ready to go.

Upon leaving her room, she noticed that the door to Jonas's room was closed. Figuring he was getting ready, she made her way back downstairs to wait. Wandering through the dining area, she went out the French doors to find Jemma and Trey playing with an adorable yellow curly-haired dog.

"Goldie, this way. Follow me," Trey was saying as he scampered around the yard. The puppy followed, attempting to pounce on Trey's heels. Trey's laughter was infectious, and she found herself wishing for what Jemma had.

"Hi, Bella. Meet Trey and Goldie." Jemma rose to her feet. "Jazz and Dalton are bringing Chinese for lunch if you're interested."

"Oh, no, really, I can't keep bumming meals off you." Bella suspected Jemma was trying to throw her and Jonas together, so she decided against mentioning they were driving into town in the same vehicle.

Carpooling. Saving gas and the environment. Right? Right.

"It's no bother," Jemma insisted. "Dalton and Jazz always buy enough to feed a small army."

"I take it your sister doesn't like to cook?"

Jemma laughed. "You got that right. Not that she can't cook, but she sees it as a chore. We have a deal, I cook breakfasts and dinners, while she and Dalton spring for lunch. It's the least I can do considering all the work they're doing on the garage apartment for me."

Bella caught a whiff of Jonas's aftershave as he came up behind her. "Well, I'll grab something to eat in town, no need to worry about me. See you later."

Bella turned and moved to step around Jonas. He stayed back, saying something to his sister that she didn't quite catch because of Trey's squeals of excitement.

"Wait up," Jonas said.

She paused and waited for him to catch up. "Ready?"

"Sure."

The interior of the car was stifling from sitting in the sun. She cranked the air and opened the windows while Jonas stashed his crutches in the back seat, then slid in beside her.

There was an awkward silence as she pulled out of the parking area and out onto the highway.

"Who was the guy who showed up last night?"

"Dr. Eli Hackbarth. But I don't want to talk about it."

"Is he a surgeon?"

"What part of not talking about it didn't you understand?" She knew she sounded testy, but this wasn't a topic open for discussion. Time to change the subject. "I'm planning to park by the quilt shop if that's okay with you. I don't know where the art supply store is located, but I can drop you off along the way."

"Look out," Jonas said. A large, lumbering tractor pulled out from a driveway hidden by trees. She pushed on the brake, but the pedal went straight to the floor.

"What in the world?" Tightening her grip on the steering wheel, she quickly pumped her foot up and down on the brake pedal.

Still nothing.

In the distance she could see a car on the horizon coming from the opposite direction on the two-lane highway, so she couldn't go around the tractor. There was no way to avoid a collision. She cast a quick glance at Jonas. "The brakes are out!"

His expression turned grim. "Aim for the farmer's field."

She did as he suggested, wrenching the wheel to the side, narrowly missing the tractor. But they were going way too fast, trees were flying past her as the car picked up speed. Upon leaving the road, the car bounced up and down wildly, then jackknifed, flipping over onto the hood.

The airbag blew into her face blinding her. Pain hit hard, then everything went dark.

CHAPTER FIVE

Jonas groaned and peered through the cloud of dust from the airbag deployment. His entire body ached. The shoulder and lap harness of the seat belt cut painfully into his torso, and it took a moment to realize he was hanging upside down.

They both were.

Bella appeared to be unconscious. Concern for her spurred him into action. Refusing to be hampered by his disability, Jonas reached down to brace the palm of one hand on the interior roof of the car. With the other, he released the seat belt.

Collapsing on the ground, he winced as pain shot up his injured leg. The constant throbbing pain he'd learned to live with had turned into a fierce blaze of agony. Ignoring it wasn't easy, but on his hands and knees, he inched toward Bella.

"Bella? Can you hear me?" He reached up and gently placed his fingers along the side of her neck, feeling for a pulse. For several long seconds he didn't feel anything, but then palpated the rapid beat of her heart. He let out his pent-up breath in a whoosh.

"Huh?" Her eyelids fluttered, then opened, revealing her clear blue eyes. Up close he could see a narrow yellow ring around the dark pupils. "What happened?"

"We flipped over. Do you hurt anywhere?"

"Everywhere," she whispered. She flexed her wrists and ankles. "I don't think I have any broken bones. My head hurts, though."

He braced her with his hand. "I'm going to release the seat belt, okay?"

"Yes." She was more docile than he liked, and he ridiculously found himself longing for the sharp edge of her tongue.

The belt gave way, and she literally dropped on top of him. He closed his arms around her, swallowing a muffled groan of agony as her foot kicked the lower part of his left leg.

"Sorry," she murmured, trying to put distance between them. There wasn't a lot of space in the crushed vehicle, but they managed to get untangled.

"We need to get out of here." He didn't like being confined in the cramped space, it reminded him of the caves in Afghanistan. Using his elbow, he knocked out the remaining bits of broken glass from the passenger side window.

"Where's my phone?" Bella was looking around the interior of the upside-down car in confusion. The contents of her purse were strewn about.

"Leave it. I have mine." He maneuvered his upper torso toward the window. His body was larger than hers, and if anyone was to be cut by remnants of glass, he wanted it to be him.

By the time he was outside the vehicle, sitting in the farmer's field, he could hear the shrill sound of a police siren. The tractor driver must have called it in. He reached in to help Bella wiggle out through the broken window.

"I don't understand what happened." She pushed her dark hair out of her face. "My brakes were fine on the trip here to McNally Bay from Battle Creek. And yesterday when I drove into town."

While Jonas knew brakes could fail at any time, he didn't believe for one minute that this was a random accident. "The surgeon you don't want to talk about must have had something to do with this."

"Dr. Hackbarth?" Disbelief laced her tone. "Are you kidding? The man wouldn't risk soiling his precious surgeon hands to mess with my brakes. And that's assuming he even knows anything about cars. He's the type to take his car in to a mechanic, not work on it himself. Besides, he showed up wearing a three-thousand-dollar suit."

Three thousand for a suit? Talk about crazy! Although now that she mentioned it, Jonas couldn't deny her impression of Hackbarth, he'd thought the same thing. "I don't like the coincidence of his arriving and your car brakes going out."

She sighed. "I know, the timing is suspicious."

He swiveled around to reach back into the car, searching for his crutches. He found and tugged them out. Thankfully they weren't broken, the lightweight aluminum frame looking no worse for being in a wreck. "I know you didn't want to tell me what's going on with you and that guy, but you'd better tell the cops. They need to know everything."

As he spoke, the brown squad with the Clark County Sheriff's Department logo etched along the side pulled over to the side of the highway adjacent to their crash site. He wasn't entirely surprised to recognize Jemma's fiancé, Garth Lewis, striding toward them.

"Are you both okay?" Concern darkened Garth's eyes. "There's an ambulance on the way."

"We're fine. No need for an ambulance," Bella said.

"Don't listen to her, she lost consciousness and needs to be assessed for a possible concussion." Jonas awkwardly stood, leaning heavily on his crutches for support. "Do you have a forensic garage nearby? We have reason to believe her car brakes were tampered with."

"What?" Garth's expression turned grim. "Maybe you should start at the very beginning."

Bella didn't say anything for a long moment. Jonas couldn't help being upset that she wouldn't confide in him. "I'll give you both some privacy." It wasn't easy to use the crutches to navigate the farmer's field, but he did his best, albeit slowly.

"Jonas, don't go. It's fine." Bella's voice gave him pause.

"Are you sure?" Now that she was willing to speak frankly in front of him, he was hesitant to hang around. As if by hearing her secrets she'd expect him to reveal his.

And that wasn't happening.

"Yes. To be honest, there isn't much to tell." Bella stopped for a moment, then continued, "I'm a nurse and work in the VA hospital in Battle Creek."

That much he'd already known, but he noticed Garth made a notation in his small notebook.

"We were working on a case that had been added onto the surgery schedule at the last minute. Dr. Eli Hackbarth was the orthopedic surgeon doing the procedure along with his assistant Emily Archer, and he begged me and Aaron Campbell, the surgical tech, to stay late for him. We reluctantly agreed. But things were rushed, and Dr. Hackbarth was getting in our way, moving stuff around in the room instead of leaving it to us."

There was a frustrated note in her voice, and he understood where she was coming from. It was the same way that the officers dictated to the men with boots on the ground without really knowing exactly what they faced each and every day.

"Okay, so what happened?" Garth asked.

Bella sighed. "It's hard to explain, but I'll give it my best shot. Each surgeon has a case cart, a list of supplies, meds, instruments, etc. that they'll need to use for the procedure. As I checked the patient's history, I saw that he had an allergy to penicillin, which happens to be the usual medication Dr. Hackbarth has on his case cart. I went to the pharmacy to get an antibiotic called Cipro to use instead. But somehow, during the procedure, the joint infection was cleaned out by Dr. Hackbarth, and he used the penicillin instead of the Cipro, which sent the patient into anaphylactic shock. The patient coded and died."

Jonas frowned and took a step toward her. "Are you saying this idiot surgeon is blaming you for his error?"

Bella nodded. "Yes. And his physician assistant, Emily Archer, backed up his story, claiming she saw me place the penicillin solution on his table, even though her back was turned at the time. I had the Cipro on the table, too, and didn't place the penicillin on the sterile field. I believe he must have done that and, therefore, used the wrong solution. Instead of owning his error, he blamed me. So now I'm on a paid administrative leave while the boss figures out who they're going to believe."

Jonas scowled, knowing that it wasn't likely that the hospital would take the word of a nurse over that of a surgeon. "The jerk."

"Yeah." Bella nodded. "He's a slime-bucket of the lowest level."

"I still don't understand what this has to do with your brakes failing?" Garth interrupted. "Battle Creek is three hours away. You really think his surgeon came here to mess with your car?"

"Hackbarth showed up at the B and B last evening," Jonas said. "He claimed he wanted to talk to Bella, but she refused."

"You both saw him?" Garth asked, writing down the surgeon's name. The deputy's scowl deepened. "You're right, that's not a coincidence."

"Maybe not, but I'm telling you, Hackbarth wouldn't mess up his suit by crawling beneath my car," she insisted. "And I can't imagine cute little Emily doing that either."

Jonas narrowed his gaze. "What do you mean, cute little Emily?"

Bella lifted her hands. "Hey, it's no secret Emily Archer, the physician assistant, and Hackbarth have a thing going on between them. He's married, but apparently that doesn't mean much to some people. Emily falls all over herself in an effort to make him happy." She hesitated, then added, "If you're asking me if she'd lie to cover for him? I say yes. She absolutely would."

Garth let out a low whistle. "Okay, I can see why Jonas thinks your vehicle was sabotaged. I'm no expert on cars, but from what I hear it's not easy to prove brakes have been tampered with."

"You'll need an expert, which is why I suggested a forensic auto body shop."

"Yeah, well, we don't have that in Clark County. I'll have to call in someone from Battle Creek or Kalamazoo to find one."

"Not Battle Creek," Jonas quickly interjected. "Kalamazoo is okay, but maybe you could find someone from the Chicago area? It's bigger. More options."

Garth nodded thoughtfully. "You're right." The ambulance pulled up behind the squad car. "Let the EMTs check you out, okay?"

"Bella first." Jonas wasn't taking no for an answer. Now that he knew the details behind Bella's impromptu visit to The McNallys' B&B, he wasn't sure what to think. It seemed like a stretch to go after a nurse by cutting the brake lines of her car. And how did the guy know which vehicle was hers in the first place? His vehicle had been parked there, too.

He didn't like the situation one bit. He was glad to be there to help keep her safe. Yeah, he only had one leg, but he was still a good marksman.

Time to get his Glock out from the bottom of his duffel, keep it close at hand.

He had a bad feeling he might need it.

Bella was irritated with the EMTs poking and prodding her. Yes, she had a mild concussion. So what? Her vision wasn't blurry, and she didn't feel like throwing up. Well, maybe a little but not bad enough that she felt as if she needed a trip to the local emergency department.

"I'm fine," she insisted for the third time. When the EMT frowned, she scowled right back. "I'm a nurse. I know that I have a mild concussion, and I know the proper things to do to take care of myself. Hand me your stupid waiver and I'll sign it. That way you can leave to take care of someone who needs you more than I do."

"Bella." Jonas's deep voice saying her name made her

shiver with awareness, a malady that she decided to blame on her concussion and the recent hair-raising events rather than on her ridiculous penchant for soldiers.

"I'm done here." She pushed past the EMTs. "Deputy Lewis, would you be willing to call for a car service to pick us up?"

"Car service?" The deputy flashed a wry grin. "There isn't much need for that here in McNally Bay. I'll give you and Jonas a lift back to the B and B."

She suspected Jemma would be upset with her fiancé if he didn't help out her brother, so she didn't argue. Glancing back at her upside-down car, she understood she'd need to find a rental car of some sort if she didn't want to be stuck at the B&B all day and all night for the next nine days straight.

Despite Jonas's suspicions, she didn't really think Eli Hackbarth had anything to do with her brakes failing. The man wouldn't dirty his fingernails, and it was a stretch to imagine him calling some mobster friend of his to do the dirty work.

Hey, Guido. I gotta job fer you.

The image of Dr. Hackbarth speaking in a heavy Bronx accent made her smile despite the fact that there wasn't much to be cheerful about. Thankful that she and Jonas hadn't been hurt in the wreck, for sure. But there was no reason to smile when her car was obviously totaled, an added expense she didn't need when her career was on the line.

Enough. She pulled herself together. Maybe her concussion was worse than she thought.

"Take my cell number," Garth said, drawing her attention to the issue at hand.

She didn't think she'd have a reason to call him directly

but entered his number into the phone she'd rescued from the car wreck. The screen was cracked, but it still worked.

"Ready to head back?" Garth asked when she'd finished.

"Sure." She followed the deputy to his car, slowing her pace when she realized how Jonas was struggling on the uneven turf.

"Go ahead. I'll catch up." His tone was terse, and beads of sweat dotted his brow. For all his insistence on her being checked out, she knew the roles should have been reversed. He'd taken a bad fall the day before and now this. She had no doubt the wound on his torso was bleeding again, although it was difficult to tell since he was wearing a black T-shirt.

And based on the grimace etched on his features, she knew his left leg was killing him.

"Listen, I'm sorry I didn't say anything about Hackbarth and our patient sooner. I don't formally have an attorney, but my friend who is a lawyer advised me not to talk about it."

Jonas grunted, and she took that to mean he understood.

They walked in silence for a few minutes when the tip of his crutch slid off a rock. He lurched sideways toward her, and she caught him with her body, holding him steady.

He stopped for a moment, his head down as if he were glaring at the rock that dared trip him up. When he finally lifted his gaze, she could see the way he had his jaw clenched with barely restrained frustration and anger.

"Hey, it's a farmer's field. The rock didn't jump into your path on purpose." She strove for a light tone, hoping to ease the tension. "But if you want me to stomp on it for you, I will."

He blew out a heavy breath, and she thought his jaw relaxed a bit. "I'm fine."

"I know. So am I."

That made him shake his head as if unsure what to think. She could relate. He knocked her off balance just by being in close proximity and breathing the same air.

Jonas resumed the laborious task of crutching over the ruts. She kept close to his left side, silently supporting him. She took it as a positive sign that Jonas didn't tell her to go on ahead.

Garth was on the phone waiting for them by the time they reached the road. Jonas leaned against the vehicle, setting the crutches aside and resting his arms.

"Don't tell me you already blabbed to my sister," Jonas said, glaring at his future brother-in-law.

"Yep. And if you think I'm sorry, I'm not." Garth opened the back of the police vehicle. "I love Jemma, and she deserves to know what happened here. By the way, she's thankful you're both okay."

"Now she'll hover worse than ever," Jonas muttered as he slid into the back seat.

"Yes, she will, but only because she loves you." Bella placed the crutches along the floor, then took a seat beside him.

Jonas didn't respond but relaxed into the seat. He lifted the hem of his T-shirt to wipe the sweat off his face, providing a glimpse of his taut six-pack abs and the blood-stained dressing on his left side.

A part of her wanted to reach out toward the dressing, but her gaze fixated for a moment on his abs. She forced herself to look away. The man was far too attractive for his own good. Too bad he was lugging around more baggage than your average 747.

As soon as the thought formed, she felt ashamed. Because it wasn't true. Granted, Jonas was struggling to adapt to life with one good leg, but she was fairly certain he'd use a prosthetic device and work through his issues without a problem.

Greg had died six months ago, and it had been another seven months since she'd last seen him. Still, they'd been engaged. She'd promised to love him, to marry him. She shouldn't be interested in a guy. Any guy.

Especially a wounded warrior like Jonas.

Jemma was waiting at the door when Garth pulled into the B&B parking lot. Bella expected Jonas to make some sort of comment about his sister's penchant for hovering, but when she glanced at him, his head was tipped back and his eyes were closed.

Sleeping? A glance at his fingers curled into fists convinced her he was attempting to internalize his pain rather than resting.

"Jonas! Bella! Are you all right?"

At the sound of Jemma's voice, Jonas opened his eyes. She was impressed that he managed not to grimace or scowl at his sister.

"We're fine." His tone was gruff and didn't invite further conversation.

"I let Jazz and Dalton know to add more to the lunch order of Chinese." Jemma's gaze bounced between them, as if searching for signs of injury. "You two should go up and get some rest. I'll let you know when lunch arrives."

"I'm sorry we couldn't get your art supplies, Jonas." Bella slid out of the vehicle first, then pulled out the crutches, holding them ready for Jonas. "We can try again later in your car if you'd like."

"Art supplies?" Jemma echoed. "You should have told me. I found some of Grandma's art supplies in the attic. The paint isn't any good after all these years, but I found two sketch pads, a broken easel, a package of charcoal sticks, and colored pencils."

There was a flicker of interest in Jonas's eyes as he took the crutches. "I wouldn't mind taking a look at what you found."

"I'll get them right away." If Jemma could have beamed herself into the attic in an instant, Bella was sure she would have. Anything to please her brother.

"It's no rush." Jonas looked tired, as if picking up a colored pencil would take too much energy.

"I have ibuprofen in my room," Bella offered as they headed inside.

"Me, too. I'll be fine." He didn't look at her, and she wondered if his desire to paint her had vanished in the wake of the crash.

She couldn't necessarily blame him for wanting distance. After all, he'd almost gotten killed simply by being in the same car with her.

At the top of the stairs, they moved away toward their respective rooms. Bella was planning to take another shower. At the rate she was going through clothes she'd need to find a laundromat in town. Once she was cleaned up, she'd head outside with her latest thriller.

Her gaze landed on her first aid kit. Knowing Jonas needed to replace the blood-stained dressing on his torso, she carried it to his room. She listened to make sure he wasn't showering, then knocked.

The door swung open revealing Jonas standing in the doorway with his crutches, a black gun tucked into a belt holster on his right side.

"What are you doing with that?" she demanded, automatically taking a step backward.

He lifted a brow. "Have you forgotten that someone just tried to kill you?"

She couldn't look away from the weapon. Despite how she'd gotten engaged to a soldier and had a brother who'd served in the armed forces, she wasn't fond of guns.

Okay, make that she had a strong aversion to guns. To weapons of any kind. Another reason she wouldn't have lasted long in the Army.

She forced herself to meet his gaze. "For all we know the brakes failed because the car is old or because I hit something on the highway."

"You don't really believe that."

She wasn't about to admit anything. Even if someone had tampered with her car, she wanted to believe it was a scare tactic, nothing more. "Here, take the first aid kit. You need it more than I do." She turned to go back to her own room.

"Bella."

The tone of his voice compelled her to look back at him. "What?"

"I won't let anything happen to you." His brown gaze was so serious and intense, she felt the impact sizzle through her.

Once a warrior, always a warrior.

She stared at him for a long moment. On one hand she was grateful to have his support, but the idea that she needed protection at all was unnerving.

"Thanks." She tried to smile, then quickly escaped to her room.

This so-called vacation wasn't turning out at all as she'd planned.

And worse? She had no desire to leave.

CHAPTER SIX

Jonas showered, changed his dressing, downed four ibuprofen, and stretched out on the bed to rest. He'd thought four hours of therapy was enough to prepare him for being out on his own, but the bone-deep exhaustion proved otherwise.

He must have slept because he woke up to an incessant tapping on his door. "What?" he asked, his voice husky with sleep.

"Lunch is ready." Jemma's muffled voice came from the other side of the doorway.

He almost declined her offer, but then realized his stomach was growling, despite the large breakfast he'd shared with Bella. Interesting that his appetite had returned. "Be down in a minute."

"Okay."

Jonas sat on the edge of the bed and raked his hand through his scruffy hair. He hadn't bothered to get it cut since his injury, but now felt self-conscious about his appearance. Not because of Bella, but Jazz and Dalton's wedding was coming up and he needed to look nice for that.

He made a mental note to visit one of those cheap hair-cut places when he returned to the VA on Friday to pick up his prosthesis.

He washed up in the bathroom and hesitated when it came to putting the belt holster back on. Bella's antagonistic reaction toward the weapon had surprised him, but he'd meant what he said. No way was he going to risk anything happening to her.

After a brief internal debate, he slipped the gun into the holster, then headed downstairs. Jazz, Dalton, Jemma, Garth, Trey, and Bella were already at the table. Once again the only empty spot was next to Bella, but he didn't really mind. Propping his crutches against the wall, he slid in beside her, appreciating the hint of strawberry he could smell on her hair and skin.

She glared momentarily at the gun but didn't say anything.

The scent of sweet and sour chicken, soy sauce, and rice was tantalizing. He was hungry and eagerly helped himself as the white containers of Chinese takeout were passed around. The conversation revolved around the status of the garage apartment construction project.

"The drywall in the two bedrooms is ready to be spackled and painted," Dalton was saying. "The open-concept kitchen and living room is almost ready, too."

"Who's putting up the new tile in the bathroom?" Jemma asked as she cut up pieces of chicken for Trey.

"Me." Jazz raised her hand with a cheeky grin. "Now that I've been practicing, I'm better than Dalton."

"Yeah, you pretend you're better at tiling than I am, but we both know you just want me to do the heavy lifting putting in the new countertops and cabinets," Dalton retorted.

Jazz laughed and gave him a quick kiss. "You're so smart. That must be why I love you."

"I can paint," Jemma offered. "After all, it's going to be my space."

"We have guests arriving the day after tomorrow," Jazz reminded her. "No need to worry, we'll handle the painting."

"Can I paint?" Trey asked.

Jemma and Garth exchanged a look. "How about if you draw a pretty picture for us to hang on our wall instead?" Jemma suggested. "We need pictures to decorate for when we move in."

Trey seemed to consider this option and nodded. "Okay."

"I'm happy to help paint the walls," Bella offered.

"Me too," Jonas added.

"Bella, I'm going to end up comping your room rate if you keep insisting on helping out." Jemma's expression mirrored exasperation.

Bella waved a hand. "Consider it payment for the meals you keep providing for me."

Jonas still wanted a chance to draw Bella and tried not to show his disappointment. He glanced at Dalton. "Do you have all the painting supplies? We can start after lunch."

"It won't be ready to paint until tomorrow," Dalton told him. "Jazz is going to spackle this afternoon, and we'll need to wait for it to dry."

"Perfect." He popped a piece of broccoli in his mouth to hide his satisfaction. This afternoon he'd convince Bella to sit for him so he could get a few sketches done. It had been a long time since he'd done any drawing, for all he knew what little skill he may have once possessed was long gone.

"Bella, did you call your insurance company about your car?" Garth asked.

She nodded. "They want a copy of the police report faxed over to them. I was hoping you could help me with that."

"Of course." Garth's expression turned serious. "I took pictures of the damage, and I'll include them with the report. I also arranged to have your car towed to a forensic garage just outside of Chicago."

"Forensic garage?" Jazz picked up on the term, her sharp gaze raking over him. "Why?"

There was a long moment of silence before Bella spoke. "My brakes failed. I'm sure it's nothing, but Garth and Jonas wanted the car to be examined by experts just to be safe."

"Does this have anything to do with that guy who showed up here wanting to talk to you?" Jemma asked.

"I think so, yes." Jonas sent each of his future brothers-in-law a pointed look. "We need to be on alert for anything else out of the ordinary."

"We will," Garth and Dalton said in unison.

"I guess that explains why Jonas is armed and dangerous," Jemma said with a sigh.

"I hope you have a permit to carry the Glock," Garth drawled.

"I do."

"Listen, I don't want to put any of you in danger." Bella abruptly jumped to her feet. "I think it might be best if I leave."

"Using what vehicle?" Jonas asked.

She hesitated and frowned. "I'm sure I can get my insurance company to pay for a rental."

"Oh, please don't leave." Jemma looked upset at the notion. "You're safer here than off on your own."

Jonas took Bella's hand and gently tugged her back down. She didn't resist but didn't look happy about it either.

"We'll talk about your options later, okay? For now, let's finish eating lunch."

Bella picked at her food. When everyone else was finished, she jumped up to help clear the table. Since it was difficult to carry dishes while using crutches, Jonas stayed where he was and combined the leftovers into a few cardboard containers.

"Oh, Jonas, here are the supplies I found in the attic." Jemma set two large sketchbooks and a container of chalk next to him. "I hope this is enough for you to get started."

"It's great." He flashed her a genuine smile. "Thanks, Jemma."

His sister gave him an impulsive hug. "I'm so happy you're here, Jonas."

"Me, too." He patted her back, catching a glimpse of Bella watching them from the counter. The yearning expression on her face made him realize how much she must miss her brother. The one who'd died in Afghanistan.

He couldn't seem to tear his gaze from hers. He longed to capture that look on canvas. With oil paint, not just a charcoal sketch.

What was it about her that called to him? That had him so tuned in to her emotions? That made him yearn for something more?

He didn't want Bella to leave the B&B. For the first time since his injury, he was looking forward to the future.

Bella finished helping Jemma in the kitchen, far too aware of Jonas lingering at the kitchen table, watching her. She tried to tell herself it was in the best interests of the

McNallys, especially Jazz, Jemma, and Trey, that she should leave. Find another place to stay.

But she didn't want to. Weirdly enough, she'd begun to feel as if she belonged here. As if she'd already become good friends with the McNallys.

Even Jonas.

Especially Jonas.

Whoa, back up. No can do. Absolutely, positively not something she should even consider.

Jonas wasn't looking for a relationship and neither was she. End of story.

She swiped her hands on her faded jean shorts and subtly left the kitchen area, picking up her thriller from the counter. She walked through the dining room and outside to the gazebo.

The lapping waves on the shoreline were mesmerizing and soothing. She closed her eyes and focused on the sound, drawing in a deep breath and letting it out slowly. The tension eased from her body, although the nagging headache from her mild concussion still lingered.

A cool breeze off the lake washed over her.

This is why she'd come to the B&B. To find a place to relax, to explore, and to figure out what her next career move should be. But ever since Garth had brought up the forensic mechanic, she'd been troubled by the possible danger she was bringing to the McNally doorstep.

She knew Garth spent a lot of time here with Jemma and Trey, but he couldn't be here 24/7. And his presence hadn't prevented someone from messing with her brake line.

If anyone had tampered with it at all.

She needed to call her insurance company back to ask about getting access to a rental.

A whiff of Jonas's spicy aftershave made her realize she

wasn't alone. She opened her eyes, blinked, and found him sitting next to her with a sketch pad on his lap. He had a dark piece of something in his hand that looked like chalk, and he was drawing lines on the page, but he was turned in a way she couldn't see what he was doing.

How he'd managed to sneak up on her while using crutches, she had no idea.

"You look beautiful." His husky voice sent shivers of awareness rippling over her skin.

"Thank you." She felt her cheeks go hot at the compliment. She wasn't used to men saying things like that to her. She and Greg had grown up together, and while she'd known he loved and cared about her, he wasn't the type of guy to say things like that out of the blue.

"Tell me about yourself," Jonas invited as he sketched.

She shifted uncomfortably in her seat. "I thought I had to stay motionless."

"I'm out of practice, so this is just doodling."

She had a feeling his doodling was far different from hers. She could do a decent cartoon character but that was about it. "There's nothing to tell."

"Where did you grow up?"

"In Dearborn, a suburb of Detroit. I attended college at Wayne State University."

"Did you always want to be a nurse?"

She nodded. "My mom was a nurse, so yes, that was always my plan. My brother, Ryan, didn't like school very much, so that's what drew him to the Army."

"Where are your parents now?" The way Jonas sidestepped the issue of her brother dying in Afghanistan irked her.

"Dead." She didn't try to soften her tone. "Where are yours?"

"Also dead."

She flinched and winced. She hadn't considered the possibility that they had that much in common. "I'm sorry."

"Me, too. For you and for me." Jonas didn't meet her gaze but remained intent on his sketch. Despite her initial aversion to being the subject of a drawing or painting, she found she was curious about what the sketch might look like.

"How long have you worked at the VA in Battle Creek?"

"Three years. I took a job there after Greg and Ryan were sent overseas. I thought it would help me feel closer to them in some way."

Jonas didn't say anything for a long moment. "Who's Greg?"

"My fiancé." Her gaze dropped to her ringless left hand. Greg had asked her to marry him prior to his deployment and she'd agreed, but he hadn't given her an engagement ring. At the time, the lack hadn't made her feel any less committed, but now she couldn't help wondering if they would have survived the long-distance relationship.

Greg's death made it a moot point. Yet these were the thoughts she tortured herself with late at night when sleep refused to come.

"I see." Jonas stopped sketching, and he stared at her with a grim frown. "You should have said something earlier."

"Like what?" It took a moment for his reaction to sink in. "I would have said something, but Greg died in Afghanistan, too. Just a few months after Ryan."

He picked up the sketch pad again. "I'm sorry. I shouldn't have been such a jerk to you when we first met."

"No, you shouldn't have been," she agreed. They met for the first time yesterday, but for some reason, it seemed more like several weeks ago.

Freaky.

"My girlfriend dumped me the moment she found out about my amputation."

"I'm sorry you had to go through that, but she's obviously not worth your time."

His eyebrow lifted. "Why is that?"

"Some soldiers come back with physical injuries, some come back with psychological injuries, and others with both. Love isn't always easy. What happened to staying together in sickness and in health?"

"But we hadn't exchanged those vows." He still didn't look up at her but appeared to be concentrating on his sketch.

The one she was dying to see.

"I know, and that's why she wasn't worth your time." She hesitated, then added, "When did you propose?"

"I didn't." He shrugged. "Looking back, it was probably for the best."

"What's the female version of a slime-bucket?" She pretended to think. "Slima-buckatee?"

He chuckled. "You're goofy."

"Yeah, I get that a lot." She smiled, glad she was able to make him laugh. It wasn't a full from-the-gut belly laugh, but it was a start.

She shifted in her seat again. The plastic deck chairs were practical for sitting out in the weather but not exactly comfortable. "Are you almost finished? I can't sit here for much longer."

"Then why did you bring a book out with you?"

Her gaze dropped to the book she'd completely forgotten about. "I don't know. Reading usually helps me relax but not today. My headache is bothering me more than I anticipated."

"You should have gone to the hospital."

"You didn't go either."

"I guess that makes us both stubborn, huh?" Jonas made a few more sweeping marks, then abruptly turned the sketch pad so she could see what he'd drawn. "What do you think?"

Bella gaped in surprise. The likeness Jonas had done of her was uncanny. For one thing, he made her look amazing, far better than the face she normally saw every morning in the mirror. But the way he'd drawn her face was incredible. He'd captured her smile, yet there was a shadow of sadness in her eyes. As if she were thinking bittersweet thoughts.

Of Greg and Ryan.

"Oh, Jonas. I had no idea you were so talented!" She couldn't tear her gaze from his sketch.

The corner of his mouth quirked in a smile. "Does that mean you like it?"

"I do, very much. It's amazing. You were far too kind to me, but I love it."

"I only draw what I see." Jonas carefully tore the sketch from the pad and handed it to her. "Now you can understand why I'd like to paint you."

"Didn't we already ascertain that I'm not good at sitting still?" She stood and set the sketch carefully on the seat of the chair, placing her book on top of it so it wouldn't blow away in the breeze. "Stand up."

"Why?" Jonas gave her a wary look as he slowly rose, balancing on his right leg.

"Because I want to hug you." She wrapped her arms around his shoulders and warmly embraced him. "This is the best present I've ever received."

Jonas's arms snaked around her waist, drawing her close.

The heat of his body ignited a simmering awareness. Unable to pull away, she tipped her head to look up at him.

"I'm glad you're not engaged," Jonas said in a low husky voice before lowering his mouth to hers.

Me, too, she thought as his kiss shot her pulse skyrocketing into orbit. She clung to his shoulders, reveling in the heat of his kiss.

"Mommy! Uncle Jonas is kissing Bella!"

Trey's voice was like a blast of cold water. She broke off from Jonas's kiss, gulping oxygen in an attempt to clear the cloud of passion that had engulfed them.

"Gee, thanks, Trey," Jonas said in a wry voice.

"I need to go." Bella took a quick step backward, belatedly realizing she'd knocked him off balance. Thankfully, he dropped back into his seat rather than falling ungainly to the floor of the gazebo.

Before he could do or say anything more, she scooped her book and the sketch in one hand, then rushed away from the gazebo.

Yet even as she went back inside to seek refuge in her room, she knew it wasn't Jonas she was running away from.

It was her own growing feelings for the wounded warrior she'd come to care about, far too much.

CHAPTER SEVEN

The impact of Bella's kiss haunted him for hours, making a mockery of the feelings he'd claimed to have for Rhonda. Bella's kiss had packed a punch, and he longed to draw her into his arms, picking up where they'd left off. It bothered him that she'd run away, even though he knew it was for the best. What did a legless former soldier have to offer a woman like Bella?

Nothing.

The following morning as Jonas showered and changed, he belatedly remembered his doctor's appointment scheduled for later that afternoon. Today was the day he'd be given his prosthesis. He was looking forward to ditching the crutches, although he was told that getting used to using the fake leg would take time, so he'd need to keep the crutches for a few weeks.

Since his appointment was for fifteen hundred hours, there was no reason he and Bella couldn't paint the bedrooms for a few hours after breakfast.

If she came down for breakfast. As he made his way

through the great room and into the dining area, he hoped to find Bella already seated at one of the tables.

She wasn't.

He frowned, propped his crutches against the wall, and dropped into a chair overlooking Lake Michigan. Bella hadn't come down for dinner the night before either. According to Jemma, Bella's headache was bothering her so she'd decided to rest.

Believable, especially since he'd noticed her sitting in the gazebo with her eyes closed that afternoon. But skipping two meals? Not acceptable.

"Good morning, Jonas." Jazz flashed a warm smile as she filled his coffee mug. "Did you sleep okay?"

"I did." Surprisingly, the nightmares hadn't plagued him since coming to the B&B. Maybe being close to his siblings had helped keep them at bay. "Have you seen Bella yet?"

"Yep. You missed her, she was up super early this morning." Jazz eyed him curiously. "I heard about the kiss on the gazebo."

He sighed. "Figures Jemma blabbed."

"Actually, Trey did."

"Great. Outed by a three-year-old."

"He's almost four," Jazz corrected. "But yeah, he told anyone who would listen how Uncle Jonas was kissing Bella."

"I'm sure Bella was thrilled to hear that." Was that why she was avoiding him? Because his nephew had opened his big mouth?

"Bella didn't seem upset this morning. In fact, she said she felt much better. Claims her headache is gone."

He nodded, glad to hear it. "Any idea what her plans are for the day?"

Jazz grinned and shook her head. "Gotta tell you, Jonas,

you have it bad, don't you? Did you forget her offer to help paint the apartment? Dalton is putting her to work as we speak."

It surprised him how anxious he was to get up into the garage apartment to see her. "Don't read anything into one kiss, Jazz. I'm sure Bella isn't interested in pursuing a relationship with an unemployed and handicapped ex-soldier. I'll have the full Irish breakfast, thanks."

"Don't underestimate her," Jazz warned. "I'm pretty sure she can hold her own, especially with a surly ex-soldier turned artist. And you're crazy if you think you have nothing to offer."

Without giving him a chance to respond, Jazz returned to the kitchen, no doubt giving Jemma his breakfast order.

Watching the boats on the lake, Jonas sipped his coffee. His sister was trying to make him feel better, but he knew the truth. The sailboat skimming across the surface was a painful reminder of the physical limitations he was stuck with. Okay, yeah, maybe he'd never sailed before, but now it was just one more thing to add to the list of things he'd never be able to do.

Sensing he was growing morose, he gave himself a mental shake. He was here. Alive. Unlike many others he'd served with. Time to focus on what he could accomplish, not on what he couldn't.

When Jazz brought him a plate of raspberry muffins, he took a big bite, savoring the tartness. He eyed his watch, hoping Jemma would hurry up with his breakfast so that he could head up to the apartment garage to help paint. A job he normally hated yet sounded fun as long as he was working alongside Bella.

Jazz was right. He had it bad.

Thirty minutes later, he stumped his way up the staircase to the garage apartment. Eighties music blared, making him wince. Why on earth Jazz enjoyed that era was beyond him.

The construction appeared to be moving at a rapid pace. He and Bella hadn't helped yesterday afternoon, but it was clear Jazz and Dalton had worked their fingers to the bone. The drywall mudding was completely finished, and Jazz was already adding the spackle and primer in the open-concept kitchen and living room.

Hence the awful music. "It looks amazing." He had to shout the compliment to be heard over the noise.

Jazz glanced over at him and smiled. "Thanks. Dalton is anxious to get this place finished so we can go back to working on our house."

He admired how Dalton and Jazz put Jemma's and Trey's needs before their own. "You still owe me a tour."

"Plenty of time. Dalton is picking up the cabinets from the hardware store. If you're looking for Bella, she's painting Jemma's room."

With a quick nod, he made his way through the construction area to the furthest of the two bedrooms. Bella was indeed painting the walls a pale yellow color, his sister's favorite, while tapping her foot to the beat of Jazz's eighties tunes.

"I thought you preferred rock and roll?"

He must have startled her because she fumbled with the roller in her hand as she spun around to face him. "I do. But Jazz's music is better than Dalton's."

Raking his gaze over her face, he was forced to admit she looked well rested. Maybe it was the headache that had kept her locked in her room, rather than their heated kiss.

But then she quickly turned and resumed painting,

concentrating on the task in a way that made him suspect she was bothered by his presence.

Feeling grim, he crossed over and picked up another roller brush. "I'll start on this end, and we'll meet in the middle."

"Okay."

For all his talk about being able to help, it soon became evident that painting while using crutches was awkward and laborious. After bending and straightening and almost falling twice, he filled another container with paint and slid it on the ladder.

"New plan. I'll do the upper half while you do the lower." Balancing his weight on his good leg, he was able to brace himself against the ladder enough to roll paint on the upper half of the wall.

"Sounds good." Bella's noncommittal responses were beginning to annoy him.

She was acting as if the kiss had never happened. Or worse, would never happen again.

They painted in silence for a good ten minutes until he couldn't stand it a second longer. "I have a doctor's appointment at the VA this afternoon to get my prosthesis."

"You do?" That caught her attention. "That's wonderful news."

"Yeah, as long as I can figure out how to use it." He'd been warned it was no easy task learning to walk on a fake leg. "I wouldn't mind some company on the three-hour drive."

There was a long pause before she nodded. "I'm happy to ride along."

"Thanks." He shouldn't be so thrilled that she'd agreed to accompany him on the long ride to Battle Creek and back. "I'm hoping to stop and pick up some oil paints and canvasses while we're there."

She sent him a sidelong glance. "Do you only draw people? Or do you do landscapes, too?"

"I've done both," he admitted. "Landscapes are easy. I prefer the challenge of painting people."

She blushed and looked away. Bella was so beautiful, and he knew he could never really do her justice with his sketches and paints.

But that didn't stop him from wanting to try.

They worked companionably for the next two hours. It irked him that he didn't make nearly as much progress as Bella did, but he tried not to let his limitations depress him. At least he was doing something useful, even if it was half of what a normal person could accomplish in the same amount of time.

By eleven in the morning, when they'd finished the first coat of Jemma's room, they quit for the day. Jazz insisted on washing the brushes, rollers, and pans while they changed their paint-speckled clothes.

"Oh, and I want you to take my truck." Jazz tossed him the keys. "Dalton has been using it without a problem, and it's been locked up in our garage at night. Don't worry, it's an automatic transmission, no clutch."

He stared at the keys in his hand, nodding soberly. He'd examined his car for signs of tampering without seeing anything obvious. But after the near fatal crash yesterday, he wasn't willing to take any chances. There was a slight oil leak, a good excuse to get a mechanic from town out to look at it, just to be sure.

"Do you want me to drive?" Bella asked as they approached Jazz's cherry red truck.

"I'd rather if you don't mind."

Her expression mirrored relief. "Trust me, I'm happy to let you take the wheel. This thing is huge."

"Safer," he pointed out.

"Probably." She settled into the passenger seat and clicked her seat belt into place. "Our seat belts saved our lives yesterday."

"I know." Neither one of them spoke for several long moments as he drove down the highway right past the scene of their recent crash.

The near miss was sobering. He'd been depressed after losing his lower leg, but now he realized just how much he wanted to live.

Not just exist day to day. But to really live a full life.

He glanced at Bella. Was it crazy to think Jazz was right? That he might have something to offer a woman like Bella?

Maybe it was time to find out.

Bella was acutely aware of Jonas's musky scent. Images of their incredible kiss flashed in her mind.

Last night, she'd convinced herself that she needed to stay away. To remain nothing more than friends. So why on earth had she jumped at the chance to ride along with him to his appointment? It wasn't as if she really wanted to go back to the Battle Creek VA Hospital. The place where she likely no longer had a job.

"What made you go into surgical nursing?" Jonas asked as if reading her mind.

It was a loaded question, one she debated whether or not to answer. "I used to work on the surgical floor, where the patients came after surgery. It wasn't until after I lost

Greg and Ryan that I made the transfer to work in the operating room."

There was a long pause. "I imagine it's less emotionally draining working with patients who are under anesthesia."

She winced. "Yeah, that was my goal. The soldiers recovering from surgery had every right to be upset about their injuries. Of course, they needed to go through the grieving process. But soon—I just couldn't deal with it any longer. It all became too much."

"I can see that." Jonas didn't seem put off by her answer. "I was a grizzly with a sore paw when I came out of surgery. Mad at everyone and everything."

Remembering how he'd been during their first meeting, she nodded. "I don't blame you, or anyone else. But for me, I would have given anything to have Ryan home even if that meant returning without one of his limbs."

Jonas sent her a sidelong glance. "That's easy to say, Bella, but completely different when you have to live with those limitations day after day."

"Nothing worth having is easy." She tried to soften the edge to her tone. "I know what you're saying, Jonas. Do you think I haven't noticed how you struggle? Yet when it came to the car crash, you didn't hesitate to pull me out of the wreck. Not only were you amazing, but you supported me when I needed you. Don't you see? That's all that matters."

Jonas didn't answer but reached out to give her hand a gentle squeeze.

She didn't pull away, enjoying the warmth of his fingers cradling hers. Holding hands with him wasn't part of the plan, but it occurred to her that it had been a long time since she'd allowed anyone to get close.

Maybe that was why she'd had such an overwhelming reaction to his kiss.

Nah. She stared at their clasped hands. She'd been asked out several times by co-workers and friends, but she hadn't been remotely interested.

Not until Jonas.

They stopped for lunch on the way, and she noticed that people stared at Jonas, some with pity, others with curiosity. A few pulled their gaze away as if they were repulsed. She began to get annoyed on his behalf.

"How do you stand it?" she asked as they slid into a booth.

He shrugged. "Not much I can do about it."

"Stupid people," she muttered.

That made the corner of his mouth quirk, hinting at a smile. "Not everyone is like you, Bella."

"Me?" Her brows levered up and then drew together in a frown. "I don't follow."

"The first day we met, you didn't once look at my deformed leg. No matter how much I goaded you, you didn't look."

"First of all, your leg isn't deformed. It was amputated because of an injury. Secondly, I see people on crutches or in wheelchairs every day, it's not that unusual." It was her turn to smile. "I will admit that the way you demanded I look at it was a unique approach. I can be just as stubborn as you."

"I figured that out," he replied dryly. "Anyway, it was the first time someone looked at me, as a person, not my injury. It was different from what I'd ever experienced before."

"Oh, Jonas." Hearing him say things like that made her heart ache. "It will be better once you get your prosthesis."

"Hope so."

They finished their meal and went back out to Jazz's truck. They were only thirty miles outside of Battle Creek, and the closer they got to the VA hospital, the more her stomach knotted with anxiety.

Her boss told her to stay away from the facility while she was on administrative leave, so being here with Jonas wasn't a smart move on her part. But his appointment was with rehab services, which was located on the other side of the building from the operating rooms. So what if someone saw her on the campus? She was accompanying a friend to an appointment, nothing more.

Still, as the stately brown brick building loomed before them, she swallowed a wave of nausea. In that moment it was clear she'd never be able to return to work. The patient's tragic death wasn't her fault, but even knowing the staff would speculate that she was guilty if she didn't return, she just couldn't do it. The only person who'd supported her after that day was Chrissy, and still, she hadn't heard from her friend in days.

She'd have to find somewhere else to live and work. Good thing her lease was almost up on her apartment. At least she wouldn't have to try to sell a house before moving on.

But she would need a new car. Or rather, a replacement one, since her old car hadn't been worth very much according to her insurance agent.

"You okay?"

She glanced at Jonas and forced a smile. "Sure."

He cocked a brow indicating he didn't believe her but dropped the subject. He parked the truck, and they made their way inside the building.

A petite blonde wearing scrubs was walking toward them. When she saw Bella, she stopped abruptly, her mouth dropping open, gaping like a fish, her eyes wide with surprise.

"You—what are you doing here?" Emily Archer's voice was an octave higher than normal, and the pure shock on her face was almost comical.

"None of your business." Bella tipped her chin, meeting Dr. Hackbarth's physician assistant's stare head-on. "A better question would be what are you doing here? This is the rehab clinic area and nowhere near the OR."

"I—" Emily abruptly spun on her heel and hurried away in the opposite direction.

"What a flake." Bella watched the young woman's retreating figure. "How can anyone get lost where they work?"

Jonas leaned on his crutches, his brow furrowed in a deep frown. "I don't think she got lost. She acted more like she saw a ghost."

"What do you mean?" It took a moment for his meaning to sink in. "Me? I'm the ghost?"

"If she was the one responsible for cutting your brake line, then yeah. Exactly." Jonas pinned her with his dark gaze. "She was surprised to see you alive and well."

A chill rippled down her arms, and she crossed them over her chest. No way. She couldn't believe it.

But as they made their way to the clinic, she couldn't shake the image of Emily's shocked expression from her mind.

CHAPTER EIGHT

Jonas couldn't erase the stunned expression on Emily Archer's face when she saw Bella. He wasn't a cop, but he wanted desperately to run a background check on the woman. Logically, he knew she must not have a criminal record or she wouldn't be working at a VA hospital, but she'd still looked guilty.

Of having an affair with a married man?

Of sabotaging Bella's brakes?

Or both?

He was glad to leave Bella in the clinic waiting room as he went to talk to the rehab doc. When the physician came in accompanied by a therapist holding his prosthesis, the fake leg that had the potential to provide a new level of freedom, his heart began to thud in alarm. He'd been told it would take time for him to learn how to walk with the new leg.

What if he couldn't do this?

Dr. Harris examined him, pronounced him fit enough to use the prosthesis, and left him alone with Allan the physical therapist.

"This is called a transtibial prosthesis. It's been custom fit for you and should fit like a glove. Ready to give it a try?" Allan asked with a grin. "I'm going to wrap your limb with an ACE wrap so we can check the fit here. After that, we'll head over to the therapy gym to try standing and maybe taking a step or two."

His gut knotted with tension, but he nodded. Allan went through the mechanics of how the prosthesis worked and how to attach it to his left leg. He went on to explain that the footwear could be exchanged for a sneaker, dress shoe, etc. for whatever occasion he needed.

Thinking of Jazz's wedding made him realize he needed to get his dress shoes out of his storage locker. He supposed he'd also have to get a suit. He couldn't wear his dress blues now that he'd been given a medical discharge from the Army.

"How does this feel?" Allan asked, looking up at him expectantly.

Truthfully, it felt awkward and strange, but he forced a smile. "Great."

"Okay, I'm going to take it off now, and we'll head over to the therapy gym. We like to start you off between the parallel bars."

He hadn't realized this appointment would take this long and wondered if he should tell Bella to leave for a while. The thought of her going off alone bothered him, so he held off.

For all he knew this could be a colossal failure.

The therapy gym was conveniently located around the corner from the clinic. When they were situated right in front of the parallel bars, Allan instructed him to put the prosthesis on.

Fumbling with the straps, Jonas realized he should have

paid closer attention to what the therapist had done. He finally had it situated and blew out a breath. "I'm ready."

"Good. Hold on to the parallel bars and stand up on your two feet. A big part of this is learning to balance on your new leg. Remember your knee works fine, you'll just have to get used to how to walk using the new foot."

He stood, savoring the moment. To test himself, he let go of the parallel bars and instantly felt himself losing his balance. He grabbed them again, mentally kicking himself for being an idiot.

"Slow and steady," Allan advised. "Once you get the hang of it, you'll be great. It takes a while to get the hang of keeping your balance. Let's try taking two steps while holding on to the bars. Lead with your prosthesis."

It galled him to have to use the parallel bars to stand and walk but did as Allan requested. The first step didn't seem too bad, but the second one, shifting his weight to the fake leg while moving his good foot forward was much harder.

Yep. A colossal failure.

"Not bad," Allan said as if reading his mind. "Do it again."

Jonas took another two steps, trying to find the rhythm. It wasn't as difficult to take the steps while supporting the bulk of his weight on the parallel bars, but he yearned to walk independently.

By the time he reached the other side of the parallel bars, beads of sweat dotted his brow.

It shouldn't be this difficult to walk a straight line. How would he manage going up the stairs to the B&B? Or the stairs to the second-floor apartment?

"Do it again," Allan said. "And this time, try not to lean on your arms so much."

A wave of despair washed over him. With an effort, he

shoved it aside. He'd survived basic training and almost eighteen months of Afghanistan.

He could do this.

He would do this.

Failure was not an option.

Jonas awkwardly turned, almost falling flat on his face, then walked the length of the parallel bars again. And again. After the fourth time, he thought it might be getting easier.

Or maybe he was delusional.

"That's all for today," Allan said when he'd finished yet a fifth stretch of the bars. "You don't want to overdo it on your first day."

"I'm going again. I don't plan on leaving here in a wheelchair or with crutches," Jonas said between clenched teeth. "I'm walking out of here under my own power."

Allan lifted a brow. "So you're one of those, huh?"

He scowled. "One of what?"

"Macho guys who think they can leap tall buildings with a single bound."

"I just want to walk, not leap tall buildings." He didn't find humor in Allan's assessment.

The therapist sighed. "Listen to me. If you try to walk out of here without any assistive devices, you'll set your recovery back several weeks. Your lower leg will blister under the constant pressure, and you'll end up having more surgery. You can't go from using crutches to walking on your new leg twelve hours a day. You gotta trust me on this."

He stared down at his fake leg for a long moment, doing his best to regain his composure. Allan was probably right. He'd been told the recovery process would be slow. He just hadn't figured it would be quite this bad.

Finally, he lifted his gaze to Allan's. "Fine. What are my options?"

"Since you have an aversion to wheelchairs, you can take the crutches or a set of canes. I would suggest you practice walking with the crutches or canes twice a day, morning and evening. Use the crutches for the time in between. Don't overdo it. I'll need you to come to therapy three times a week, starting Monday."

Jonas winced, three times a week with a total of six hours of travel time would be difficult. But not impossible. After Jazz's wedding, he could find a place to live in Battle Creek, just until he could walk independently.

"Okay." He straightened and began to walk the length of the parallel bars for the last time. He moved slowly, trying to use the bars for balance more than for holding his weight. When he reached the other end, he caught a glimpse of Bella hovering in the doorway of the gym.

She was watching him with bright eyes and a broad smile.

A feeling of accomplishment welled in his chest, and he smiled back at her. He couldn't be angry that she'd come to find him after waiting over an hour. The joyous expression on her face was exactly what he'd needed.

If Jemma had been here, he knew she'd be crying all over him. But not Bella. From the very first time they'd met she'd acted different toward him. No sympathy. No pity. In fact, she flat out told him to get over himself.

Bella saw his efforts as a sign of progress. Maybe it was her nursing background combined with her recent losses that made her act differently toward him.

Whatever it was, he liked it. Liked her.

And was forced to secretly acknowledge how much he'd miss her when their time together at the B&B was over.

～

Jonas was walking!

Bella could barely contain herself. She wanted to leap into the air doing a wild fist pump but thought that might be overdoing it.

Jonas would surely figure out that her feelings for him were morphing into something more than simple friendship.

Her problem, not his. Still, watching him maneuver through the parallel bars was the highlight of her day.

Stumbling across Emily Archer in the hallway an hour earlier had been the lowest point.

While she'd waited in the uncomfortable plastic chair, she'd replayed their accidental meeting over and over in her mind. She didn't want to believe Jonas was right. That the pure shock that had flashed in her eyes hadn't been because Bella had been alive and well.

It just didn't make any sense. Even if Emily and Hackbarth were having a hot affair, it had nothing to do with the medication error the surgeon had made.

It seemed unlikely that Emily would do something so drastic as to tamper with her brakes in hopes of injuring her. Bella wasn't a threat to the surgeon. The hospital was already leaning toward Eli Hackbarth's side of the story. Especially since both Emily and Aaron Campbell had agreed with his assessment of what had taken place.

No. The more she thought about it, the more she had to assume that Emily had been surprised to see her at the hospital while being on a paid administrative leave of absence. Or maybe Emily had been on her way to some secret liaison with Hackbarth. Bella remembered there were call rooms located on the lower level of the clinic area.

Yep. That was it. A secret rendezvous had to be the source of the PA's guilt.

After playing endless games on her phone, she'd decided to find out how much longer Jonas would be. Finding him in the therapy gym had been easy, and she'd watched him for long moments as he'd mustered his strength and determination to walk on his new leg.

"Looking good." She approached the parallel bars, noticing how the physical therapist eyed her curiously. "How much longer will you be?"

"He's finished for the day." The therapist wore a name tag that identified him as Allan. "Sit down for a minute, Jonas. Remember what I said about overdoing things?"

The way Jonas glanced at her she knew he didn't want her to watch him take the leg off, so she turned away. "I'll be in the waiting room when you're ready. And I found an art supply store nearby, too."

Without waiting for a response, she returned to the uncomfortable plastic chair. She brought up her map application to verify the art supply store was only five minutes away.

Not far from her apartment. She grimaced and wondered if she should just go ahead and break her lease now. After the past few days, she'd lost her zest for returning to her job. What was the point? Even if her name was cleared, which was doubtful, people would always look at her and wonder. Hospital gossip traveled faster than the speed of light. She could already imagine the whispers and snickers that would dog her heels like a shadow.

Her reputation had already taken a hit. Her chance of recovering from that was slim.

"You ready to get out of here?" Jonas's voice was low and strained. She glanced up at him, noticing the lines of exhaustion that bracketed his mouth. She'd heard from her patients that an hour of physical therapy could feel like running a half marathon. He had the crutches again and was wearing a backpack, which she knew held his prosthesis.

"Of course." She slid her phone into her purse and stood. "I was thinking we could go to the art supply store, then stop at my place for a little bit. I need more old clothes that I don't mind getting stained with paint."

"Sounds like a plan." Was it her imagination or was there relief in his dark eyes?

"I also have ibuprofen if you need some." She led the way back to the parking garage where they'd left his car. "And I don't mind driving, I know the area better than you do."

"Okay." Jonas must have been hurting because he didn't utter a protest. He stored his crutches and backpack in the back, then slid into the passenger seat of Jazz's truck.

Rush hour traffic in Battle Creek wasn't like in Detroit, but it still took fifteen minutes to get to the art supply store. Jonas appeared eager to go inside, and she was glad they could do something to make him happy.

She followed him to the oil paints and canvas area, watching with bemusement as he filled the cart. Her eyes popped when she saw how much he spent.

"Wow. Pricey." She carried the bag out to the car.

"It's an initial investment. Other than the canvasses."

She glanced at him when they were once again settled in the car. "My apartment is just a half mile away. It's close to dinnertime, I figured we could order takeout and eat there before driving back to McNally Bay."

"I'd like that." The exhaustion lacing his tone was more pronounced.

She drove the short distance to her apartment building, parking in her underground spot so that it would be easier for Jonas to get to the elevator. Her apartment was on the third floor, and after a grueling PT session, she knew the elevator was their best bet.

Ten minutes later, they were walking into her apartment. Jonas looked around curiously. "Nice place."

"Yeah, I guess." Oddly enough it no longer felt like home. Which was strange since she'd lived there for going on four years. "I, uh, thought we'd order subs, unless you'd rather do pizza."

"Subs are great." Jonas made his way over to her sofa and sat down with a low groan. "I have to put my leg up for a while."

She nodded and pulled out her phone. "What kind do you want?"

"Roast beef."

Bella place the order, choosing turkey for herself, then rummaged in her fridge for soft drinks. "I have iced tea, lemonade, or water. Unfortunately for you, I gave up diet sodas two years ago."

"Water is fine." Jonas had his head tipped back on the cushion, his eyes closed. She set the water on the end table beside him, then went into her bedroom to find more old clothes that she wouldn't mind getting ruined.

She took her time, thinking Jonas might need a power nap. But when she returned to the living area, he was sipping his water, staring out through the living room window at the brown brick hospital building that was visible from here.

"I'm supposed to attend therapy three days a week," he said, breaking the silence.

She wasn't surprised. "You'll do great. From what I saw today, it's clear you'll be walking on your new leg in no time."

The corner of his mouth tipped up in a half smile. "It's a workout for sure. But I was thinking about the six-hour round-trip drive. Seems a little crazy."

Realization dawned and she felt her cheeks flush with embarrassment that she hadn't understood what he was getting at. "Oh, and you'd like to stay here? Of course, you're more than welcome."

Jonas shifted on the sofa as if seeking a more comfortable position. "I don't want to invade your space. I can sleep right here on the couch."

Her cheeks were burning now, and she quickly looked away. "That's not a problem. I'll be happy to give you a key." She jumped up and hurried into the kitchen, rummaging through her junk drawer for her spare set.

"Here." She dropped them in his lap. "Use the place any time."

He picked up the keys, eyeing her curiously. "Thanks. But I wasn't thinking I'd be here alone. You live here, right?"

Dear heaven, could her face get any hotter? He wasn't asking to move in with her, but that's how she was acting.

Get a grip, Bella.

Thankfully, the buzzer indicating their meal had arrived prevented her from making a fool of herself. She hurried over and pressed the lock, allowing the delivery person to come in.

"I have it," Jonas said, pulling bills out of his wallet.

She wanted to protest, but the steely glint in his eye warned her off. She reluctantly took the cash and opened the door.

They ate at her small kitchen table. He jutted his chin at the framed picture sitting prominently on the end table. "Your brother? Or your former fiancé?"

"My brother, Ryan." Sadness welled in her chest, and she did her best to shake it off. "I miss him."

Jonas nodded solemnly. "I can't imagine losing one of my siblings. They drive me nuts, but I love them."

"I remember you saying something about having a lot of siblings."

"Yeah, there's six of us in all. Three brothers, all older than me, then my younger twin sisters."

"Must be nice to have such a large family." She didn't bother to hide the wistfulness in her tone.

When they finished eating, Jonas made his way back into the living room to stretch out on the sofa again. She suspected his left leg was hurting and went to get the promised ibuprofen.

"Let me know when you're ready to drive back."

He nodded, but then closed his eyes. Leaving him alone for a bit, she pulled out her laptop computer and began searching for a new job. She applied for several jobs in the southern Chicago area, this time steering away from surgical nursing in the operating room. She thought it might be nice to try rehab nursing.

Jonas continued to sleep. As the hour grew later, Bella decided there was no point in driving the three hours back to The McNallys' B&B. She called Jemma to let her know she and Jonas were staying in town, explaining that the physical therapy had wiped him out and he was currently sleeping on her sofa.

Bella yawned and padded into her bedroom. She'd just changed into a comfy pair of boxer shorts and tank top when she heard a muffled thud.

Fearing Jonas may have rolled off the sofa, she hurried into the living room. Jonas was still stretched out on the sofa, apparently sound asleep.

Reminding herself that she was surrounded by other apartments which could account for the thud, she turned to head back to the bedroom.

When the door handle to her apartment jiggled, she froze, heart thudding in her chest. Slowly, she faced the door.

The handle rattled again, harder this time. There were small metallic sounds, too.

Bella forced herself to approach the door. She raised up on her tippy-toes, pressing her eye to the peephole.

She couldn't see anyone. And when the door handle jiggled again, she knew.

Someone was attempting to pick the lock!

CHAPTER NINE

"Go away or I'll call the cops!"

Bella's shout had Jonas jackknifing up from his supine position on the sofa. He looked around wildly, automatically reaching for his weapon, before remembering he'd left it in the glove box of Jazz's truck.

"What's going on?" He grabbed his crutches and stood. "What happened?"

"I think someone was trying to break in." Bella's blue eyes were wide with fright, and he noticed she was twisting her fingers together nervously.

"What do you mean?" He crutched over to her and put his hand on her arm. Her skin felt cold and clammy, and he could tell she was literally shaking with fear.

"The door handle was jiggling, and there were metallic sounds, too. I looked through the peephole but didn't see anyone out there." She moved closer to him as if seeking comfort and protection. "That means the person outside the door was kneeling while picking the lock, right?"

"Or it was a kid, too short to be seen through the peep-hole." Pinching the crutches beneath his armpit, he pulled her close, hugging her. It was hard to believe someone would bother to break into Bella's apartment. To what end? "A kid who has the wrong apartment maybe. Like he lost his key and didn't want his parents to know."

"How do you know it's a he and not a she?" Bella wrapped her arms around his waist and buried her face against his chest. He sensed she was talking in an effort to ward off tears.

"I don't." He rested his cheek against her dark silky hair, savoring the strawberry scent. The kiss Jemma's son Trey had interrupted flashed in his mind, but he told himself that this wasn't the time or place. He needed to stay focused. "But I still think it could be a kid. Maybe he or she was trying to pick the lock on a dare. Stay here, I'll take a look."

"No!" Bella tightened her grip. "I don't want you to go out there alone."

"I might be handicapped, but I can still take care of myself."

"Don't be an idiot. You're not handicapped." She lifted her head to look up at him. "You're a trained soldier. Big difference."

He couldn't fight, but he could shoot. If he had his Glock. "I'm sure you scared off whoever was out there. I'll take a quick look." And head down to his car to get his gun, but he didn't tell her that.

"I'll go with you." Bella's tone was firm, and he inwardly sighed. He should have expected that response.

"Fine, but stay behind me." He dropped his arms, allowing her to move away.

She went to open the door, and he noticed there was no deadbolt.

"You need better locks," he chided, moving past her so

he could go into the hallway first. The entire corridor was empty, and there was no sign that anyone had been there.

"It's a safe neighborhood." Her excuse was weak, and he decided her landlord needed to install a deadbolt as soon as possible.

And if she didn't make the call, he would.

"I need to get something out of my car." He crutched toward the elevator.

"Your gun? I don't like that idea."

"I'm a trained soldier, remember?"

The trip down to Jazz's truck, then back up to Bella's apartment didn't take long. Before heading inside, he set the crutches against the wall and bent his good leg so that he could see the lock in the door more closely.

There were several small scratches around the keyhole. It wasn't definitive proof of a lock-picking attempt by any means, but it was suspicious.

"See? I told you." Bella's tone held a note of defiance.

"I know." He didn't point out that simply inserting the key into the lock could cause scratches, too. Bella had noticed the door handle jiggling and had heard metallic sounds, and he found himself believing her. And he was glad to have his Glock holstered in his belt.

What he didn't understand was motive. Why would anyone attempt to gain access to her apartment? To steal something? If so, what? She had a TV and laptop, but it wasn't as if she was living in some swanky place that reeked of money.

It didn't make any sense.

"Do you keep cash here?"

Bella locked the door behind them, then came over to join him on the sofa. "No. I barely use cash. The hospital deposits my checks automatically, and I use my debit or credit card. No need to carry money."

"Is there anything else of value here?" He persisted. "Jewelry? Rare coins? Anything worth stealing?"

She snorted and spread her hands wide. "Are you kidding? Look around. What you see is what I have."

"Do you know who lives in the apartment directly above or below you? Could be that the lock-picker had the wrong apartment."

She shook her head. "No, I don't know who lives upstairs or downstairs. I know the woman across the hall because she's a nurse at the VA, too. But even then, I don't see her often, she works night shift and I work primarily days. There's a single mom with a young girl in the apartment next to me, but she's moving out at the end of the month. There's a young couple a few doors down; they always greet me when they see me. I doubt any of them has valuables worth stealing."

"So why, then?" His brain was still a bit foggy with sleep. He'd been out for the count when she'd awoken him by shouting.

Bella blew out a heavy sigh. "You're right. There's no reason for anyone to try to break in. It must have been a kid on a dare. Or someone had the wrong apartment. Anyone could have lost their key."

He glanced at the door again, thinking about the way the female physician assistant, what was her name? Erin? No, Emily, had looked so shocked to see Bella. Emily would know that Bella was here in Battle Creek and therefore had no reason to try breaking in.

Still, Jonas didn't like the weird things that were happening around Bella. First Hackbarth showing up in McNally Bay, followed by the failed brakes. Now this latest issue here in Battle Creek. It was as if danger followed Bella wherever she went.

"I think we should hit the road." He looked her in the eye. "It's safer at the B and B than it is here."

"We can't. I already told Jemma we were staying here because you'd fallen asleep on the sofa." She flushed and looked away. "Don't worry, I made sure she knew that you were exhausted from your physical therapy appointment."

"Gee, thanks." He grimaced. "Now she'll have more to worry about."

"I didn't want her to think . . ." She didn't finish.

"That we were staying here, together as a couple, I know." He decided to hit the subject straight on. "Give me a little credit, Bella. I'm not that kind of guy."

"Oh boy." She buried her face in her hands, no doubt hiding the pinkness of her cheeks. He liked the way she blushed. "Can we please change the subject?"

He longed to pull her into his arms again, this time to kiss her until they both couldn't breathe. More proof they should drive back to McNally Bay. Not that he'd ever take advantage of Bella's kindness, but sharing the apartment suddenly seemed intimate. Even with him sleeping on the sofa.

Besides, it would be best to put distance between Bella and her potential enemies.

"Does anyone at the hospital know you live here?"

She looked surprised by the question. "I don't know, maybe. It's not a secret that many of the hospital staff live in the building. As a nurse working in the OR, I have to take call every fourth weekend, which means we need to live within thirty minutes of the facility."

"So Emily and Hackbarth both know you live here? Do you think it's possible one of them tried to break in to plant evidence of some kind?" Even as he said the words, he saw the flaw in his theory. The apartment building was six stories high and held at least twenty apartments per floor. Knowing Bella lived here wasn't enough.

The person who'd tried to break in would have to know the exact apartment number.

"Maybe." Her tone was thick with doubt. "What kind of evidence?"

He slowly shook his head. "I don't know. Drugs? Something to discredit you?" It was the only reason he could come up with, and still, it didn't make sense considering Emily had seen them that afternoon.

"Hospital investigations don't go as far as to search employees' apartments," Bella protested.

But someone could call a tip in to the police, claiming Bella was selling drugs from the place. It may be enough to get a search warrant.

Either way, they weren't staying here. "We're leaving," he said again. "Trust me, Jemma won't care if we come in late. We have keys to get in, and if we're quiet, she won't even know we're back until morning."

Bella looked indecisive for a moment, then reluctantly nodded. "All right, we'll go on one condition."

He raised a brow. "Like what?"

"You let me drive so you can rest."

A flash of annoyance caught him off guard. It was the first time since they'd met that she treated him like an invalid.

And he didn't like it.

"Forget it. I already slept. I don't need to rest." He knew he sounded testy but didn't care. "You can rest while I drive."

She looked as if she wanted to argue but didn't. Instead, she got up from the sofa and went into her bedroom. At first he thought she wasn't going to leave with him, but she returned a few minutes later with a small bag of clothes.

"Let's go, then."

"Fine." He followed her out of the apartment and waited while she locked the door. Neither one of them spoke on the elevator ride back down to the parking garage.

He put his crutches in the back, then slid behind the wheel. Bella took the seat beside him, setting her bag of clothes at her feet.

It wasn't until they were out on the highway that she spoke. "I'm sorry."

The apology caught him off guard. "For what?"

"For making it sound like you couldn't drive." She sighed and shrugged. "I'm not usually overprotective. Blame it on the weird lock-picking incident."

"It's fine." He glanced at her. "But I prefer the sharp edge of your tongue. It makes me smile."

That made her laugh. "You're a goofball."

"That's better than a slime-bucket."

The tension eased, and he noticed Bella soon used the window as a headrest, her eyes drifting shut.

As he drove through the dark night, he turned this theory over in his mind. If by some chance Emily or Hackbarth had known Bella's apartment number, it was entirely possible the lock-pick incident was related to the brake line being cut.

He needed Garth's help to investigate this latest turn of events.

They needed something to go on before things escalated any further.

Because he didn't trust the arrogant surgeon or the pretty blonde PA any farther than he could throw them.

Bella slept during the ride back to the B&B, waking as Jonas pulled into the driveway. "I slept the whole way?"

"Pretty much." He smiled, and she was glad Jonas seemed to have forgiven her. "Remember we have to be quiet so we don't wake Jemma and Trey."

"I know." She climbed out of the car, then reached for her clothes. She knew better than to offer to help Jonas and approached the door of the B&B to unlock it.

He crutched toward her, the backpack holding his leg hanging from his shoulders.

"Wait. I'll grab the art supplies." She walked toward the car. "Unlock it for me."

The electronic beep indicated she could open the door to Jazz's truck. She pulled out the large bag of supplies, then returned to the doorway.

They tried to be quiet as they made their way up the grand staircase. Bella's foot slipped, and she nearly dropped the bag of art supplies. She managed to hang on, but it made a thudding noise when it hit the wall.

"Shh," Jonas whispered.

"I'm trying," she whispered back. It was odd to be sneaking into the B&B after midnight, almost as if she and Jonas were teenagers who'd sneaked out to kiss by the bonfire on the beach. The image made her giggle, and she ended up hitting the bag of art supplies against the wall again.

"Are you trying to wake them up?" Jonas demanded in a hushed tone.

"No." She swallowed another laugh and tried to step carefully. How Jonas could move more silently up the stairs with his crutches than she could with two feet was beyond her.

"Who's there?"

The bright beam of a flashlight pinned them on the stairs. Bella turned and lifted a hand to deflect the glare. "Jemma? Is that you?"

"Bella? Jonas?" The light from the flashlight moved away from them. "What are you doing here?"

"We decided to come back after all." Bella didn't want to worry Jonas's sister with the strange door-rattling incident. "Sorry, we didn't mean to wake you."

"You scared me to death," Jemma admitted. "I was just about to call Garth."

"Sorry, sis." Jonas waved a hand. "Go back to sleep. We'll talk in the morning."

Jemma didn't say anything for a long moment. "Yeah, okay. See you at breakfast." The flashlight moved away down the hall, and they waited for the door to close before continuing up the staircase.

"Now you did it," Jonas whispered. "She'll want to know exactly why we decided to drive home so late."

She couldn't argue with his assessment. After all, she had been the one to bang the bag against the wall, twice. "Just tell her that my sofa was like sleeping on a pile of rocks."

He made a snorting noise while continuing his way up the stairs. He unlocked the door, flipped on the light switch, then made his way inside. She followed and stood in the center of the space uncertainly.

"Where do you want your art supplies?"

"Anywhere is fine." He shrugged out of his backpack and carefully set it on the bed. She could tell that he valued his prosthesis as much if not more than the paint and canvasses he'd recently purchased.

She decided to set the bag on the overstuffed chair in the corner of the room. It was caramel in color and looked nice against the yellow walls. The green room was great, but she found she liked the cheerfulness of the yellow.

She glanced toward the door. "If you're set, I'll see you in the morning."

"Wait."

His deep and husky tone sent goose bumps rippling over her skin. She met his gaze and knew he wanted to kiss her again.

If she were smart, she'd leave. Kissing Jonas would only get her in trouble. It would make her heart ache with longing for something she'd never have.

But her feet stayed stubbornly rooted to the floor.

Jonas picked up his crutches and came toward her. When he was close enough to touch, she came forward, eliminating the gap between them.

"Izabella." Hearing her full name only shot her pulse higher into the stratosphere. He pulled her close and lowered his mouth, capturing hers in a sweet, then increasingly passionate kiss.

She clung to his shoulders, reveling in being held against him. Desire sparked, then flamed, making her dizzy.

The butt of the gun digging in to her side brought reality crashing down.

He was a wounded soldier looking for solace. As soon as he was moving independently, he'd go on his way.

Leaving her heart broken in tiny bits behind.

"I have to go." Bella stumbled as she hurried toward the door. Before Jonas could say a word, she slipped out and closed the door behind her.

Once she was in her room, she collapsed on the side of the bed, shaking her head at her foolishness. She had no willpower when it came to resisting Jonas. He was everything she liked in a man. And he could kiss better than anyone she'd ever been with.

Even Greg. She squelched the flash of guilt. Greg was gone, and even if he wasn't, he wouldn't want her pining over him forever.

But Jonas McNally? She sighed. Loving a man like him was a sure path to heartbreak.

Time for her to move on.

CHAPTER TEN

By some miracle Jonas managed not to fall flat on his face when Bella abruptly walked away. He wasn't sure what had caused her to end the kiss, and he was tempted to go to her room and demand an explanation.

But his therapy session caught up to him, exhaustion rolling over him in waves. With a muffled groan, he stretched out on the bed and closed his eyes. Sleep didn't come easy, thanks to the impact of Bella's kiss, but he finally drifted off.

When he awoke the next morning, it was already eight o'clock. His entire body felt achy and sore, but he was determined to keep moving forward with his plan of practicing twice a day to learn how to walk without any assistive devices.

He couldn't wait to get rid the despised crutches. And in his mind, canes weren't any better. His personal, and admittedly aggressive, goal was to be able to walk down the aisle at Jazz's wedding on his own two feet.

After a quick shower, Jonas made his way down to the dining room. He'd hoped to find Bella there, but there was no sign of her. Instead, he found two couples he'd never seen before sitting at tables overlooking Lake Michigan. He'd almost forgotten that Jazz and Jemma had guests for the weekend.

Was Bella taking advantage of sleeping in? She certainly deserved it after everything that had happened, but he'd hoped to share breakfast with her again. Eating alone reminded him of the long days he'd spent in the hospital.

His stomach rumbled as Jazz came over with a pot of coffee. "Morning, Jonas. I heard you came in late last night."

Her cheeky grin made him inwardly groan. His sister was already matchmaking. If Jazz acted this way in front of Bella, she was sure to run for cover.

"I'll have the French toast." As much as he didn't want to broach the subject, he found himself asking, "Has Bella been down yet?"

"Yes. She's already up in the garage apartment, applying a second coat of paint to Jemma's room." Jazz filled his mug with coffee. "She sure is dedicated to helping us while she's on vacation."

"Yeah." He wanted to believe Bella's interest in helping was partially because of him, but he wasn't sure that was true. Bella's nature was to be a giver. He wondered if he should help paint after breakfast? They'd done well working together the day before.

Yet, it might be better to use the time while everyone else was busy to practice walking on his prosthesis.

"French toast coming up." Jazz winked at him. "You're gonna love it. Jemma's French toast is a big favorite. Most of the reviews on our website specifically mention it as a reason they'd come back to visit."

"Sounds great." He sipped his coffee, listening as the couple closest to him made plans to rent a sailboat for the day. A bittersweet reminder of what he was no longer capable of doing.

At least, not yet. Maybe someday.

He had to learn to walk first.

Jazz returned with cinnamon rolls that melted on his tongue. He hoped Garth knew how lucky he was to have Jemma and that he appreciated his sister's talent in the kitchen.

He stopped at one cinnamon roll because gaining too much weight might throw off the fit of his new prosthesis.

The French toast more than lived up to Jazz's praise. He was proud of his twin sisters for the new business they'd started. It would clearly be a huge success.

When he finished his meal, he took his time sipping one last cup of coffee, thinking about where he could practice walking. He needed an open space with a smooth surface. Eventually he'd need to learn how to walk on uneven surfaces, he'd noticed there were brochures in the waiting room that had shown men with one leg climbing mountains for Pete's sake, but for now, he thought it best to heed his therapists advice by taking things one step at a time.

Maybe in the garage? It was certainly big enough, and the concrete floor was smooth. The only problem was that it wasn't very private with the family and Bella working right overhead.

He wasn't keen on the idea of having an audience.

"More coffee?" Jazz held up the pot.

"No thanks." But seeing her gave him an idea. "Do you have time to give me that tour of your new place? The old Stevenson house?"

Jazz glanced around the dining room, verifying the two other couples had already left. "I'd love to. Let me check on

Jemma first. We'll do the tour before I get to work on the apartment garage."

"Thanks." If the place was gutted, the way Jemma had indicated a few nights ago, then it might be the perfect place for him to practice without anyone watching. He only needed an hour. Remembering how difficult it had been to walk between two parallel bars, he figured using the crutches for support would be easy enough.

Jazz returned a few minutes later. "Jemma is fine. Let's go." Jazz's smile and gleam in her eye gave him the impression she was eager to show the place off.

Jazz led him down the driveway, probably thinking that it was easier with his crutches than cutting across the yard. As they approached the house, it was easy to see the neglect in the peeled paint, faded and missing roof shingles, and gaping cracks around the windows. Except for the second floor, where there were brand-new windows lined with white vinyl siding.

"It's a work in progress," Jazz warned as she punched in a code to unlock the door. He watched over her shoulder, memorizing the number sequence.

The door swung open revealing a wide open area with an open staircase, not as grand as their grandparents' home but very nice. He noted there wasn't carpet or other flooring, just sheets of plywood lining the entire area.

"This is going to be the kitchen and open-concept living room," Jazz was saying. "A powder room will be along the back side of the staircase, and there are four bedrooms upstairs."

"Looks like a similar layout to Grandma and Grandpa's place," he noted.

"Kind of." She waved a hand. "Only flip-flopped. We wanted the seating area to look out over the lake. So guests will walk into the kitchen here, and then follow it through to the living area. Our goal was to maximize the view."

"Perfect," he agreed.

"Dalton designed it. He's an architect by background, but these days he prefers to renovate houses."

Remembering how they'd worked together in the garage apartment, he nodded. "You two make a great team."

Jazz gave him an impulsive hug, nearly knocking him off balance. "I'm glad to hear you say that. I love him so much. I'm thrilled you've come for our wedding."

He patted her back. "Wouldn't miss it."

She broke away and glanced at the staircase. "The master suite is finished if you'd like to take a look."

"Sure." He laboriously followed her up the stairs, going much slower since he could only do one step at a time, but when he entered the master suite, a huge room with a four-poster king-sized bed done in blues and greens, he let out a whistle of appreciation. "This is incredible!"

"Thanks. Our hard work paid off." Jazz opened the door to the bathroom, revealing a space that was almost as big as the yellow room he was currently staying in. There was a claw bathtub and shower stall with gleaming tile and glass walls. The green and blue color theme was in here, too, in muted tones.

"Impressive. You and Dalton did all the work yourself?"

"Yep." She opened the glass shower door, waving a hand at the interior of the shower. "And this is what makes me the queen of tile. Okay, Dalton helped at first, but I'm a quick learner and finished this up all by myself."

He chuckled remembering the good-natured ribbing she and Dalton had exchanged the day before. "You obviously deserve to wear the crown."

That made her laugh. She led the way back to the lower

level, picking up stray nails from the floor as she waited for him.

"I, uh, have some exercises to do." He felt awkward asking but didn't want to use the space without her permission. "Would you mind if I used this area for a couple hours per day? I won't get in your way."

"Of course not!" She rattled off the code he'd already memorized. "Help yourself. We've been spending a lot of time in the garage apartment because Jemma and Trey deserve to have their own space. We won't do any more work in here until that project is done."

He understood her rationale and followed her back outside. "Thanks."

Thirty minutes later, Jonas let himself back into Jazz and Dalton's house with his backpack. He looked around for something to sit on, realizing he hadn't thought it through. A place to sit so he could put his prosthesis on would be nice, but he decided to make the best of it.

Ten minutes later, he was standing on both legs. So far, so good. He wanted to walk without the crutches but forced himself to walk with them, remembering Allan's coaching as he went. Surprisingly, using the crutches was easier than the bars, probably because he was used to them. He did a second pass, then carefully turned and propped them against the wall.

Time to try on his own. Taking a deep breath in, he stepped forward with his fake leg. He held his arms out at his sides, like a tightrope walker in the circus. He brought his good leg forward and managed to stay upright.

Buoyed by his success, he did it again, only this time when he put his weight on his fake leg, he lurched to the left and fell hard onto the plywood. Splinters of wood poked into his skin and pain rippled up his leg. He clenched his jaw against the wave of agony and stared morosely up at the ceiling.

Feeling like a complete and utter failure.

~

Bella was surprised Jonas hadn't come to the garage apartment to help paint but resisted asking Jazz or Dalton where he was.

After breaking away from their heated kiss the night before, she wasn't so sure Jonas was in the mood to talk to her anyway. Running away like a schoolgirl had been foolish, yet she knew remaining in Jonas's embrace was asking for trouble.

She hadn't slept well, her thoughts whirling around the strange incident at her apartment and the devastating impact of Jonas's kiss. Her emotions were already far too tangled up with him, and she knew that the more time they spent together, the harder it would be to get over him when it was time to move on.

There was no doubt in her mind that she'd have to relocate in order to get a new job. In fact, she needed to interview now, before the Battle Creek VA took any action against her. For all she knew, they'd report her to the Michigan State Board of Nursing for negligence.

She tightened her grip on the paintbrush, fighting off a wave of panic. Fighting the state board would take time and money. She wasn't destitute, but moving to a new location would take a large chunk out of her savings. And who knew how long it would take to get through the human resources red tape of interviewing and starting a new job? In her experience, the process could easily take a month, maybe longer.

Pushing the worrisome thoughts away with an effort,

she concentrated on painting. Doing the work alone wasn't nearly as much fun as it had been yesterday, sharing the task with Jonas. It was humbling to realize that her desire to be near Jonas was the main reason she'd agreed to help out in the first place. How selfish was that?

After she finished one entire wall, she took a quick break, walking into the open kitchen living area to find Dalton mounting the beautiful white kitchen cabinets. Easy to see the place was going to look spectacular when they were finished.

"Have you seen Jonas?"

"Nope." Dalton finished drilling the cabinet into place before glancing over at her. "I've been working since seven thirty the minute both sets of guests came down for breakfast. Jazz was helping Jemma; she may have seen him."

Bella felt her face flush. "Oh, it's no big deal, I was just curious. Seems the work is taking much longer without his help."

Dalton cocked an eyebrow. "You don't have to help at all, Bella. After all, you're on vacation, right?"

She nodded and looked away from his curious gaze. She didn't want to explain why she was on a paid leave of absence from the hospital. Jonas knew, but she didn't want the rest of the McNally clan to look at her differently after hearing about the medication error that caused a patient in her care to die. It pained her to know that even though she hadn't made the error, she was still involved just by being part of the operating room team. "I am on vacation but didn't have any specific plans. I don't mind lending a hand."

Without giving Dalton a chance to say anything more, she returned to the bedroom to resume painting. Once she'd finished the second coat, she could always excuse herself from the project. No reason to keep sticking around

McNally Bay. She could easily head southwest to find a new place to live and work. It was probably a better use of her time off anyway.

Then again, her insurance company hadn't responded to her request for a rental car. Another expense to erode her savings account. There was nothing she could do about it now, and she decided to ask Jonas for a ride to a rental car agency after lunch.

She had only gotten halfway through the next wall when Jazz came to find her. "Hey, will you do me a favor?"

"Sure." Bella set her paint roller down. "What do you need?"

Jazz grimaced. "Jonas is doing some sort of therapy in our place, and I'm worried because he's been in there for a while now. Would you mind checking on him?"

Bella hesitated, not sure Jonas would like the intrusion. Knowing it was better for her to do it than his sisters, she nodded. "Sure thing. I was going to take a bathroom break anyway."

"Here's the code." Jazz rattled off four numbers. "Thanks, Bella."

She repeated the number sequence in her mind as she descended the stairs to ground level. After a quick bathroom stop, she walked over to the rather run-down looking house.

After punching in the four numbers, she opened the door, peering through the narrow opening. "Jonas? You in here?"

There was a loud thumping sound. Pushing through the doorway, she raked her gaze over the area, finding Jonas lying on the plywood floor. He had his prosthesis on, but it was clear that he'd tried and failed to walk without any assistive devices.

Her instincts were to rush to his side to check for

injuries, but she held herself back with an effort. "Need a hand?"

"No. And I don't need an audience either." His tone was sharp, his face pulled together in a grimace of anger mixed with frustration.

"How many times have you fallen?" She kept her tone matter-of-fact.

"Three. Not that I'm counting." He ignored her and half-crawled over to the wall where he'd left his crutches.

The open space wasn't set up like a therapy gym, and she knew Jonas shouldn't be doing this alone. At the very least, someone should be there to hand him his crutches and to make sure he didn't break any bones.

Without saying anything, she crossed over to grab the crutches. She handed one of them to him, waiting for him to use it as a prop to rise back up to his feet.

Sweat had dampened the sides of his face, mixing with sawdust to create streaks of dirt. He ground his teeth together as he leaned heavily on the crutch to lever himself upright.

"You could use a spotter." She kept her tone mild. "It's not smart to do a workout on your own."

"I already told you, I don't want or need an audience."

"A spotter is someone who helps keep you on track. Someone who can prevent you from doing more harm than good. You've already fallen three times. Do you really want to add a fourth?"

Jonas avoided her gaze as he shakily stood. "I'll fall as many times as I have to in order to walk again."

Her heart squeezed at the desperate determination in his tone. She wanted to hug him but knew he'd only rebuff any display of sympathy.

"How about if I walk along your left side? That way, if

you start to lose your balance, you have someone to grab on to."

He braced himself on the crutches, staring at the floor for a long moment. Finally, he lifted his gaze to hers. "I'm heavier than you. I'll knock you over."

"I'm stronger than I look." She waited, holding her breath while his desire to walk wrestled against his need to be alone.

"Fine." Using the crutches, he walked over to the wall, turned, and propped them against the drywall. "Let's see if it works."

Bella nodded and took up a position along his left side. He moved his prosthetic leg forward. Then there was a brief hesitation as he shifted his weight onto his prosthesis for the second step.

He tilted toward her, and she held out her arm for him. He lightly grasped her arm, steadied himself, then completed the motion.

The tense lines around his mouth lessened a bit as he stayed upright with just the slightest pressure on her arm. Jonas took another step, then another. Each time, he used her to stay balanced. Sometimes he leaned harder on her than others, but by the end, he was hardly holding on to her at all.

When they reached the other side of the room, he let out a heavy sigh. "It worked."

She couldn't help but smile. "I'm glad. Every weight lifter knows you need a good spotter."

The corner of his mouth quirked in a half smile. "I wish I would have thought about that sooner. I could have used the wall the same way. I can't tell you how many splinters I have from hitting the plywood."

His dark brown eyes locked on hers, and the simmering attraction she'd tried so hard to ignore flared between them.

"Jonas." She let out a pent-up breath. "I don't—we shouldn't—this can't go anywhere."

Stark disappointment flashed in his gaze. But it was gone so quickly she thought it may have only been her imagination.

"I, um, you're right. Thanks for the help, but I think I'm done for the day." He leaned against the wall. "Do you mind grabbing my crutches for me?"

She did as he asked, carrying them over. "So, what are your plans for the rest of the day?"

"I'd like to set up my canvas, easel, and paints. Thought I'd start with painting the lake, since I'm sure my skills are rusty." He stood for a moment, giving her the impression he wanted her to leave. "Maybe I'll see you later."

It was her turn to feel the sharp stab of disappointment. "Yeah, sure." She left, hurrying back to the garage apartment.

It appeared Jonas was no longer interested in painting her portrait. Something she hadn't been all that excited about in the first place but that now seemed like a missed opportunity.

Battling a sense of loss, Bella threw herself into painting Jemma's bedroom, putting thoughts of Jonas and the relationship that could never be out of her mind once and for all.

CHAPTER ELEVEN

Bella Collins was going to be the death of him.

Jonas watched her walk out the door of Jazz and Dalton's house, feeling as desolate as if she were walking out of his life for good.

The idea of never seeing her again put a hollow feeling in his gut. He'd only known her four days, and by some strange quirk of fate, Bella managed to weave her way into the threads of his life.

With an inward sigh, he reminded himself that he shouldn't get emotionally involved. No way was Bella interested in a relationship with a handicapped ex-solider turned amateur artist.

He removed the prosthesis, noting a small area of skin on his lower leg that looked red and sore. No doubt from one of his many falls. He massaged the area, hoping to minimize any potential skin damage.

Allan had warned him against doing too much too soon, but he'd given in to his stubborn impatience. Now he feared he may have only prolonged his recovery.

For a moment the magnitude of what lay ahead overwhelmed him. How long before he could live a normal life? Sure, he was getting some Army pay, but that wouldn't last forever. He needed to contribute to society. Sitting around and doing nothing wasn't in his nature.

Glancing through the windows of Jazz's home, the blue water shimmered and rippled in the breeze. The waves beckoned, and he knew he needed to set up his canvas and paints to find a sense of peace.

Less than thirty minutes later, he was sitting on one of the plastic chairs from the gazebo with his sketchpad on his lap. There were dozens of boats on the water, but he focused on the small sailboat that bobbed on top of the waves, not far from shore. From his vantage point, the figure manning the boat looked to be a teenage boy. He thought about what he'd been like as a teenager, happy and carefree.

Jonas couldn't regret his decision to serve his country. He still felt strongly that it was the right thing to do. But it wasn't easy to come to grips with the price he'd paid for that service.

As he sketched, the knot in his chest loosened and his tense shoulder muscles relaxed. When it was time to use the paints, he experienced a wave of anticipation, something that had been lacking for a long time.

Time slipped past without his being aware of it. The painting took shape on the canvas, and while it wasn't technically great, he liked the way the blues of the water met the sky. He'd captured the sailboat cresting a wave, the sail tipping crazily to one side.

"It's so beautiful, Jonas."

Startled, he glance over his shoulder to see Jemma standing behind him. "It's a start," he said, knowing her opinion, much like his own, was biased. "I'm grateful you found Grandma's sketching supplies."

"I have the easel, too, but Dalton is fixing it. He'll have it ready for you after lunch." Jemma took a step toward him. "I wish I could draw or paint so I could capture the expression of intense serenity on your face."

He felt the tips of his ears turn red. Time to change the subject. "Did you say something about lunch?"

"Yes, I've made minestrone soup with sandwiches. Nothing fancy. Should be ready in thirty minutes."

"Sounds good. I'll be in shortly."

Jemma nodded but didn't leave.

He glanced over at her and lifted a brow. "What is it?"

"I just wanted to tell you how much better you look since the day you arrived. I think being here with us has been good for you and—I want you to stay, Jonas. I've been thinking that once I move into the garage apartment, you could take over the master suite."

"That's a kind offer, Jem," he said, choosing his words carefully. "And I appreciate the opportunity, but I need to attend therapy in Battle Creek three times a week, so it makes more sense for me to find a place there, at least for the short term."

"But don't you see? That's perfect!" Jemma's eyes lit up. "By the time you're finished with therapy, we'll be moved in. You can take over the master suite and we'll still have six rooms to rent."

He didn't want to burst her bubble, but the idea of sticking around McNally Bay didn't appeal. He still needed to figure out what kind of job he could do with a prosthetic leg. There wouldn't be much of an opportunity in a small town.

"Please, Jonas?" Jemma's voice softened. "I want you to be happy."

"I'll think about it." He couldn't lie to her, yet he didn't want to upset her either. He and Jemma had the same color-ing, and they'd always been close as kids. "Give me some time, okay?"

"Take all the time you need." Jemma's beaming smile made him inwardly wince. She'd be so disappointed when he left. But maybe he wouldn't have to go far. As long as he was close enough to visit, they'd be able to stay in touch.

"Mommy!" Trey's voice intermingled with the sound of a dog barking. A golden ball of fur came barreling toward him.

"I can't remember if you met Goldie," Jemma said when the golden ball of fur jumped into his lap to lick him. "She belongs to Jazz and Dalton, but Trey gets to help take care of her. It's the perfect arrangement."

"She's cute." He avoided Goldie's attempt to lick him in the face by cradling her in his hands and scratching behind her ears. "Goldendoodle?"

"Yep."

"Come, Goldie," Trey called.

"Don't forget to fill her water bowl," Jemma warned.

"I won't! Come, Goldie!" Trey repeated. The puppy jumped off his lap and ran happily back to Trey.

Jemma followed her son back inside, and Jonas stayed where he was for a moment. Being near his family was nice, but staying longer than the promised week wasn't part of his plan.

Granted, his plans were full of gaps these days.

When he made his way into the kitchen within the thirty-minute time frame Jem had given him, he saw that Bella was already seated at the table. She only gave him a brief glance of acknowledgment before turning her atten-tion to Garth.

"Since you're off duty today, would you mind giving me a

lift to a rental car agency?" Bella asked. "My insurance agent finally got back to me, approving the expense."

"I'll take you," Jonas interjected before Garth could answer. "I'm sure Garth has other plans for his day off."

"Let me think about that," Garth said with a crooked smile. "My choices are to work on the upstairs apartment where Jazz and Dalton order me around like some imbecile who can't pound a straight nail or drive Bella to a rental agency. Hmm. I pick the latter."

Jonas narrowed his eyes, pinning Garth with a silent plea to back off. Garth ignored him.

"Thanks, Garth, I really appreciate the lift." The way Bella smiled at his future brother-in-law had him clenching his jaw so tightly his teeth hurt. "I found one that's only an hour away, shouldn't take too much time out of your day."

Jonas wanted to yell at the top of his lungs that he's the one who should take Bella. After all, he wasn't nearly as helpful with doing construction.

"Garth, I thought you were going to help paint Trey's room now that Bella finished putting the second coat of paint on my room?" Jemma's wide gaze wasn't fooling anyone at the table. His younger sister was making her opinion clear, and he didn't think it was about the garage apartment but more about him and Bella.

For once he didn't mind Jemma's meddling. For one thing, he liked spending time with Bella. Besides, now that he'd finished the lakeshore, the next step was to attempt a portrait.

And Bella was the woman he wanted to paint.

Garth let out a heavy sigh. "Okay, okay. Bella, I hope you don't mind if I back out and let Jonas drive you instead."

"Of course not." Bella still didn't look at him, and he

could tell she wasn't thrilled with the prospect of spending time with him.

It hurt, but he did his best to ignore it.

From this point on, he needed to remember to keep his relationship with Bella in the friend category.

～

"Thanks to Bella and Jonas, the garage apartment is ahead of schedule," Jazz announced as she plopped down beside Dalton.

"Bella, not me," Jonas protested.

"Thank you, Bella." Jemma's eyes glittered with gratitude. "It's wonderful of you to help us on your time off."

"It's nothing." Bella flushed under the scrutiny of their attention and shifted in her seat. She wasn't about to admit that her initial reason for helping out was to spend time with Jonas. And look where that had sent her? Straight into an emotional minefield. "It's nice making a difference. It's one of the reasons I went into nursing."

"I bet you're an amazing nurse," Jemma said. "Your patients are lucky to have you."

Bella didn't want to talk about her career, or lack thereof, so she turned toward Garth. "Any news on what caused my brakes to fail?"

Garth grimaced and shook his head. "No, sorry. Not yet. I'll bug them again later."

She nodded, wondering if the delay meant there was foul play. Hard to believe, yet after the weird lock-picking incident, she couldn't deny it made sense.

When they'd finished eating, Bella turned toward Jonas. "Are you sure you don't mind giving me a ride?"

"I volunteered, remember?" There was a slight edge to

his tone, and she hoped the ride wouldn't be rife with tension.

At least it was only one hour one way, rather than six hours round-trip.

While she waited for Jonas, she caught a glimpse of his recent painting of the lake that Jemma had proudly displayed in the dining area on one of the tables. Bella was struck anew by his talent. He'd captured the sailboat cresting a wave perfectly, and she imagined the teenaged boy at the helm was a possible self-portrait of Jonas at the same age.

"Ready?" His deep husky voice sent her pulse thumping erratically.

She did her best not to show her reaction as she turned to face him. "Of course."

They didn't speak as they made their way outside to Jonas's four-door sedan. He automatically went to the driver's side, so she slid into the passenger seat.

The silence continued for several miles until she couldn't stand it a minute longer. "How long did it take you to paint the lake?"

He shrugged. "Three hours. I want to add more detail but need to wait for it to dry."

"Are you thinking of selling your work?"

He shook his head. "It's not good enough for anyone to pay for it. I don't think I could support myself that way. I don't know what type of job to apply for. Most soldiers end up turning to law enforcement, but that's not an option for me."

She understood his dilemma. "You can go back to school on the Army's dime, though, can't you?"

"Yeah." He frowned. "Not sure what I'd study. I've thought about teaching, but not sure I have the patience for dealing with kids all day."

The image of Jonas teaching grade school made her smile. It was so not his style. "High schoolers? You seem like the type to connect well with rebellious teens." And no doubt, the girls would all have crushes on him, she added silently.

"Maybe." He didn't sound convinced. "But if I go through four years of college and end up hating it, I'd have to start all over again."

"True." She thought about the job she'd applied for just before lunch, at the Zablocki VA Medical Center in Milwaukee, Wisconsin. They had several jobs posted on their website, and she was drawn to the area because Milwaukee was also situated on Lake Michigan. As planned, she applied for a position on the rehab unit, her second choice being a general surgical unit.

No way was she going back to working in the operating room directly with surgeons.

"Have you thought about your next step?" Jonas asked, reading her thoughts. "You mentioned the possibility of moving away from Battle Creek."

"I've applied at the Zablocki VA Medical Center in Milwaukee," she admitted.

"Milwaukee, Wisconsin? That's pretty far away. At least four hours by car, maybe more."

She shrugged. "I don't have anything holding me in Michigan. Luckily, Wisconsin is a compact license state. Meaning I don't have to sit for the nursing state board again, they'll issue me a license because I already have one in Michigan."

"I see." She sensed Jonas wasn't excited for her, yet she didn't understand why. After all, they both knew she was only staying at the B&B for a little over a week.

Maybe less, in her case. If she was able to get some traction on the job application in Milwaukee, she'd have to think about subletting her apartment or breaking her lease so she could move. She dreaded the thought of packing and then unpacking, but there wasn't an alternative.

Seeing Emily had only reinforced how terrible it would be to return to work there, even if she was able to transfer to another unit. Which was highly unlikely if the powers that be decided to fire her.

Bella knew she needed to resign her position. Better to simply take herself out of the situation and leave all the bad karma behind.

"If there's anything I can do to help, let me know."

That comment puzzled her. "You mean like a reference?"

"That or helping you move. Whatever you need. I don't think it's smart to apply for a job or even enroll in school until I'm finished with therapy."

"Um, thanks. I will. The reference will come in handy, for sure. Obviously I can't use Dr. Hackbarth."

"There must be another surgeon you work with that would stick up for you."

"A few," she admitted. "But they're not going to rock the boat. No reason for either of them to stick their neck out for a mere operating room nurse. We're a dime a dozen, right?"

"Wrong. If they were smart, the administrators there would do whatever was necessary to keep you."

Once again, Jonas had knocked her off balance. Not only because he'd become her staunch supporter, but his offer to help her move. To get a job.

Did this mean he was thinking of keeping in touch with her once their stay at the B&B had come to an end? Or was this just his way of being polite?

She had no clue. But she secretly hoped for the latter.

Friends, she reminded herself. You could never have too many friends. Jonas was a great person to spend time with. Jemma, Jazz, Dalton, and Garth, too.

But mostly Jonas.

She turned to stare out at the passing scenery, her heart squeezing painfully in her chest. She didn't want to be just friends with Jonas.

She wanted more.

"Do you know anyone who drives a black SUV?"

Jonas's abrupt question interrupted her thoughts. She looked over at him, then twisted in her seat to look through the back window.

"No, why?"

Jonas glanced at his rearview mirror, then shrugged. "Nothing. I noticed the same SUV has been behind us for the past few miles, that's all."

She wrinkled her nose. "How can you tell? Doesn't one black SUV look the same as any other?"

"Not exactly." Jonas flashed a quick smile. "But it's too far away to see the license plate, so it's probably nothing more than my naturally suspicious nature."

If it was nothing, he wouldn't have brought it up. Trusting Jonas's instincts, she shifted so that she could see the black SUV in her side mirror.

The SUV slowed down, putting more space between them.

"Even if someone was out to harm me or make me look bad, we're in your car, Jonas, not mine."

"I thought of that, but my car was parked next to yours at the B&B. And Emily saw us together. It wouldn't be impossible for someone to discover this car belongs to me."

"But how would she, or anyone else for that matter, figure out who you are? I mean, sure Dr. Hackbarth came to the B&B, but why would he assume you were another McNally? It just doesn't make any sense."

"They could look in my medical record from the VA," Jonas pointed out. "My amputation isn't easily ignored."

"But—that's illegal!" Bella was horrified just thinking about it. Then a surge of adrenaline went through her bloodstream. "And if they did, there will be an electronic trail." She pulled out her phone. "I'm going to call and request an audit report from the compliance department." She dialed, then hesitated. "Actually, I can't request an audit of your record, Jonas, but you can."

"We'll do that later." Jonas's gaze was locked on the rearview mirror. "The SUV is right on our tail."

"No way." She felt her stomach tighten with dread. Remembering how they'd rolled the car just a few days ago made her sweat. She didn't want to go through that again. "Jonas, you need to pull off at the next exit."

"Not unless there are plenty of people around," he argued, pushing the accelerator to gain more speed.

The SUV kept pace.

"I'm calling nine one one." She'd never in her life dialed the emergency number, but she didn't hesitate to do so now. The operator's voice was calmly reassuring.

"What's the nature of your emergency?"

Before Bella could speak, the SUV rammed into them from behind with enough force to cause her to drop the phone.

"Hang on," Jonas said, the muscles of his arms bunching with the effort to control the vehicle. He jerked the steering wheel and quickly crossed over to the next lane just in time to take the exit.

Bella braced herself, turning to search for an indication

that the SUV had followed them, but there was no one behind them.

In fact, there was no black SUV in sight, at all.

She put a hand over her heart. They were safe for the moment, but without a license plate or the car itself, they had no proof to back up what she and Jonas knew had happened.

CHAPTER TWELVE

Jonas pulled into the parking lot of a convenience store and gas station, shut down the car, and turned to face Bella. "Are you okay?"

She gave a shaky nod and picked her phone off the floor. He could hear a woman's raised voice on the other side of the line.

"We're fine," Bella told the dispatcher. "The danger is over."

The female voice started up again, but Bella once again assured the woman they were not hurt and disconnected from the call. "There's no point in making a report," she said in a dull voice. "The SUV who did this is long gone, and I doubt there's anything they can do to find the vehicle involved when we can't provide a license plate number."

He didn't like it but couldn't argue against her point. "Do you know if Hackbarth or Emily Archer drive a black SUV?"

"Hackbarth has a Porsche."

"This is Michigan. No matter how much money a surgeon has, no way is he driving a Porsche in the winter." Jonas thought back to the shape of the SUV. Could it have been a BMW? Maybe. "I bet he has at least two cars, maybe more."

"I have no idea what he drives," Bella said on a heavy sigh. "Even if we thought it was his car, we can't prove it. Especially since we don't know for sure who was behind the wheel."

"I know." Jonas scrubbed his hands over his face as the adrenaline faded from his bloodstream. That was way too close. And far too similar to the incident with Bella's failed brakes. "You need to call Garth. No way is this a coincidence."

Bella sighed. "I don't want to burden Garth with my problems. I doubt this area is within his jurisdiction. We're not in Clark County, are we?"

"I don't know, but I still think Garth needs to hear about this." Jonas pinned her with a stern look. "He said he'd check on the results of your car later today, right? Knowing about this recent event may convince him to push the forensic team."

Bella shrugged but didn't say anything more. Jonas swallowed a wave of frustration and pushed his door open. He swung out of the sedan, then reached for his crutches. Making his way around to the back of the car, he bent down to examine the damage.

There was a deep indentation and scuff marks along the back bumper. Anger burned in his belly. Not because of the physical damage but because of how things could have ended up being so much worse.

If he hadn't noticed the tail, he wouldn't have been prepared for the purposeful collision. And it had taken all his strength to keep the car steady and on the road. Another second later and he may have missed the exit.

There wasn't a single doubt in his mind that Hackbarth

was behind this. As Bella pointed out, he may not be doing the dirty work himself, but all these attempts against her had to be under the direct order of the maligned surgeon.

And it appeared he was getting desperate.

Bella joined him at the rear bumper, and he squelched the temptation to draw her into his arms. "I'll pay to get it fixed," she said softly.

"Don't be ridiculous. I couldn't care less about the car." His voice came out harsher than he intended, so he softened it, adding, "All that matters is that you're okay."

She gave a tiny nod, her face pale. "This is the second time I've put your life in danger, Jonas." Her blue eyes were stricken with worry. "If you were smart, you'd stay far away from me."

"That's not happening." He needed to touch her, so he leaned on his crutch and took her hand in his. "I'm not leaving you alone."

She clung to his hand for a moment. "At least having a rental car will help. Whoever is behind this won't be able to track me down."

He continued to hold her hand, unwilling to let her go. "I was thinking about that. It might be best if I rent the car under my name. We can leave my vehicle at the rental car place for a few days. That way they won't know what either one of us is driving."

"But—I still need my own vehicle," she protested. "Isn't the rental information confidential? I can't be tracked through the paperwork I fill out, right?"

He hesitated, unsure how to respond. The average person couldn't do that, but a surgeon like Hackbarth had money, and anyone could be bribed to break the law. "That's a question for Garth," he finally admitted. He gently squeezed her hand. "Please call him. For me."

Her gaze locked on his for a long moment before she reluctantly nodded. "Okay."

While she scrolled through her phone to find the number, Jonas tried to think of a way to convince her to let him rent the car under his name.

At this point, he didn't put anything past Hackbarth, even going as far as to tail them today.

"We're fine, Garth," Bella assured the deputy. "There's a dent in Jonas's car, though. We're still planning to rent a vehicle but thought you might follow up on the investigation related to my failed brakes." There was a pause, then she said, "I understand. See you later, then."

"What did Garth say?" Jonas asked. "Is he going to file a report and check on your wrecked car?"

"Yes, to both. And apparently this is still Clark County, it extends to the state border. But he admitted there isn't much to do without identifying information related to the SUV. He is calling the forensic garage right away, but as it's Saturday, he said there's no guarantee he'll get information. It's more likely to be Monday before we learn anything more." She paused, then added, "He mentioned that only a cop should be able to track my credit card purchases, like a rental car. And being a weekend, it wasn't likely anyone would be able to do that now."

He'd forgotten it was Saturday and was cheered up by the news. "Okay. Let's hit the road, I'll feel better once we have a rental vehicle."

Bella opened her mouth to say something but didn't. She returned to the passenger seat. He watched her for a moment before following suit. Five minutes later they were back on the interstate.

The rental car agency was only ten miles away. He put

his hand on her arm to hold her there. "Bella, please let me rent the car."

She shook her head, avoiding his gaze. "No, Jonas. I mean, if you want to rent one, too, that's fine. But I need to have my own vehicle. Besides, if I can be tracked through the paperwork or credit card transactions, so can you."

He didn't like how she was pulling away from him but was helpless to do anything to change it. He dropped his hand and shut down the engine. "Okay. But I'm staying behind you on the trip back to McNally Bay."

It didn't take long for Bella to obtain a vehicle, a white Honda Civic. He waited for her to pull out in front of him, then followed.

The drive back to the B&B seemed incredibly long without having Bella beside him. Once he'd craved being alone, there was never a moment of peace and quiet while in Afghanistan, but now he keenly missed Bella's companionship.

It wasn't healthy to have become this emotionally attached to a woman he'd only met a few days ago. Yet he knew it wasn't just Bella's beauty that called to him. It was her approach to life. Her positive attitude. Her ability to accept him the way he was, without making a big deal out of his disability.

The way she made him laugh.

And in the end, Jonas knew it was her laughter that would steal his heart.

Bella decided to stay at the B&B through the weekend. It wasn't smart, but since Jonas made it clear he wanted to paint her on Sunday, she gave in.

The day passed without issue. By Monday morning, Bella knew that she needed to resign from her job. While sitting for Jonas while he sketched her likeness, her mind had drifted back to the near collision on the interstate. When Jonas had questioned whether or not Hackbarth had two vehicles, she'd denied it. But sifting through her memory, she clearly remembered a day she'd been called in early for a surgery and had driven into the parking structure right behind Dr. Hackbarth.

He'd been driving a black SUV.

As crazy as it sounded, she realized that the surgeon must be lashing out at her, either in an effort to discredit her or to silence her, for good.

It wasn't worth risking her life to keep her job.

Jonas joined her for breakfast as they'd agreed to ride into Battle Creek together. His therapy appointment was scheduled for one in the afternoon.

"Jonas, I wonder if you could do us a favor before your doctor's appointment," Jazz said when she'd come in to refill their coffee.

"What do you need?"

There were no other guests at the B&B, since the two couples had left on Sunday, so Jazz didn't hesitate to drop down in a chair next to her brother. "We've been so focused on finishing Jemma's garage apartment that we forgot to tell you about the letter we found in the attic."

Bella sipped her coffee, wondering if she should excuse herself. It sounded as if Jazz wanted to talk about family stuff that didn't include her.

"What kind of letter?" Jonas asked.

"A letter to Lucy signed J. I have it here." Jazz pulled it out of her pocket and spread it on the table. "It sounds as if

Lucy died, and we're wondering if the Clark County Library may have some information about it."

Intrigued, Bella leaned forward to read the letter for herself.

Dearest Lucy,

My world is dark without you in it. I don't understand how this happened, and I'm finding it difficult to move on without you.

Life is so precious yet so brief. In one fleeting moment it's gone, as if it had never been. I've searched the Bible for answers but have found no solace to ease my pain. Some would say I haven't tried hard enough, and that may be true. It isn't easy to dissect one's mistakes, holding them up to the glaring light of day.

This suffering is my price to pay.

Always, J.

"Who in the family is named J?" Bella asked.

Jazz laughed. "Who isn't? Our dad's name was Justin, his parents, our grandparents, were Joannie and Jerry McNally. It's hard to tell from the letter how old it is, but we're leaning toward it being written by our father."

"And you have no idea who Lucy might be?"

Jazz hesitated, then shrugged. "It's hard to say for sure. Not everyone in town is happy to have us back. Old Leon Tate and his daughter Mary have made it clear there's no love lost between our families. I get the sense there were others, too. You know how it is when one family has more success than the next."

"This place was referred to as the McNally Mansion for years," Jonas agreed. "Often with disdain."

"I always wondered if the problem was with how our great-grandparents immigrated here from Ireland," Jazz agreed. "Most immigrants came with little to no money after losing everything to the potato famine, so they were in competition for jobs. On the east coast there were actually signs posted claiming, 'Irish need not apply.'" Jazz cast her gaze around the interior of the house. "I'm not sure we told you the story of how our grandparents managed to become so successful."

"What did they do for a living?" Bella asked.

"Granddad grew up on my great-grandparent's farm, but when he was old enough to be independent, he decided to open a grocery store. He met and married our grandmother, who helped out." Jazz lifted her hands palm upward. "We don't know details, but we think he bought this land along the lake for a decent price because back then there was a feeling that having property near the water was risky because of possible flooding. He was also a phenomenal carpenter, and Grandma took over running the store while Granddad began to build houses."

"So he built this place with his own two hands?" Bella was impressed.

"Yes, but not right away," Jazz said. "He built a house in town, sold it, then built another one. He did that a few times, before he began this place."

"Amazing," Bella murmured. "Still, it seems odd for your grandparents to have enemies."

"Not as crazy as you may think," Jazz argued. She gestured to the letter. "There's always a reason to be jealous. It doesn't matter now, other than to salvage our curiosity. Maybe when you have some time you can dig in to this for us. Between working on the garage apartment and last-minute wedding planning, I won't have time. This Saturday is the big day."

"I'm aware," Jonas said dryly. "Sure, I'll see what I can come up with."

"Thanks, bro." Jazz jumped to her feet. "I'd better help Jemma before she fires me."

Bella sipped her coffee, eyeing Jonas over the rim. "What do you think? We could head over to the library now, then hit the road. Should be plenty of time to make your appointment."

"Sure." Jonas stood. "I need ten minutes to grab my stuff."

They'd agreed to take her new rental car as an added precaution. When Jonas returned, he was wearing his gun on his hip and using the prosthesis along with his crutches. Bella frowned at the gun but knew it wouldn't be long before Jonas wouldn't need the crutches anymore. He was doing great.

It occurred to her that once he was back to leading a normal life, he may not need her anymore either.

Jonas used his phone to find the Clark County Library, which happened to be located in the building adjacent to the sheriff's department. Since guns weren't allowed in the library, he stored it in the glove box of the rental before they went inside.

"Good morning." The woman behind the counter beamed at them in a way that gave Bella the impression that she didn't see many patrons during the summer. "My name is Susan Harper. How can I help you?"

"I'm Jonas McNally, and I'm looking for local newspaper articles from fifty years ago, maybe longer."

Susan looked surprised. "That's a broad time frame, any particular dates or time frame?"

Jonas shrugged and glanced at her. "What do you think?"

"I think we should start with summer." It was a long shot, but considering how people hunkered down in the long winter months, she thought it was the time a tragic accident might take place.

"Sounds good. We'll start fifty years ago in June."

Susan gave them a pained look but nodded. "Okay, let me see what I can find."

"Jonas McNally, is that you?" An older woman's voice caused them to turn away from the counter. Bella didn't recognize the short plump woman with curly gray hair who smiled broadly at Jonas. "My name is Betty Cromwell, and I knew your grandparents very well. I must say, you're the spitting image of your father."

"Nice to meet you, Ms. Cromwell." Jonas held out his hand. The older woman cradled his hand with both of hers. "This is my friend Bella Collins."

They exchanged pleasantries for a few minutes before Mrs. Cromwell asked, "What brings you to the library?"

Bella was surprised when Jonas readily answered, "Ms. Harper is getting old newspaper articles for us. We're looking for information on the tragic death of a woman named Lucy."

"Lucy Tate?" Mrs. Cromwell asked. "Why are you asking about young Lucy after all these years?"

Jonas lifted his eyebrows in surprise. "Tate? You knew Lucy Tate?"

"Of course, I knew Lucy." Mrs. Cromwell appeared exasperated by his question. "Why wouldn't I? I've lived here my whole life, I know everyone. Well, except for the tourists. They come and go too often to bother keeping track of their names."

Bella exchanged a hopeful look with Jonas. This was easier than pouring through old newspaper articles through various time frames. She cleared her throat. "Mrs. Cromwell, if you don't mind us asking, what happened to her? To Lucy Tate?"

Betty Cromwell pursed her lips for a long moment as if

searching her memory. "I believe it was the summer before Lucy's junior year of high school. She would have been about sixteen. Justin McNally had gotten a new speedboat and loved taking everyone out to water-ski."

"Justin? My dad?" Jonas interrupted.

Betty nodded. "Your father was a nice boy, almost to a fault. He never said no to anyone, and trust me, there were times he should have. Some of the young men didn't hesitate to take advantage of your father's generosity."

"Go on," Bella urged. "Tell us about Lucy."

"Everyone knew Lucy had a crush on Justin, and I think he was sweet on her, too. But there were several boys in the group that were jealous of Justin's boat and the fact that he lived in the McNally Mansion. One night, oh, it had to be fifty-two years ago now or thereabouts, they took the boat out for a ride. A ride that ended badly when Lucy fell overboard."

Bella swallowed a gasp. "Did they find her?"

"Eventually, but it was too late. The official report listed it as an accidental death by drowning." Betty shook her head sadly. "Poor Leon went crazy. He blamed Justin for killing his baby sister, even though Justin was driving the boat that night, so it didn't make sense that he'd personally caused Lucy to fall into the water."

There was a long silence as the information sank in. The letter signed J made more sense now. The letter had been written by Jonas's father to his dead girlfriend.

"There's always been a hint of mystery surrounding Lucy's death," Betty continued.

"What do you mean?" Bella asked.

Betty Cromwell shrugged. "There were four boys on the boat that night, and Lucy was the only girl. There were rumors of a fight, but the boys refused to talk about it. All four of them claimed Lucy's death was an accident, and no amount of questioning made them deviate from their story."

"So why the mystery?" Jonas asked. "Sounds cut-and-dried to me."

Betty leaned forward, her voice dropping into a conspiratorial whisper. "There was an injury found on Lucy's temple. One that the medical examiner thought may have happened pre-mortem."

Bella knew that meant the bruise had to have happened prior to Lucy's drowning. She looked at Jonas.

They now knew who Lucy was and how she died, but there was obviously more to the story. Had Lucy gotten between a few of the boys who were fighting? Had one of them hit her, causing her to fall overboard?

There was no way to know what happened for sure. Which left them with more questions than answers.

CHAPTER THIRTEEN

Pre-mortem. Lucy had been struck on her temple prior to falling overboard. Jonas couldn't get the thought of Lucy Tate's death being more than just a tragic accident out of his mind. Was that part of the reason his dad had written the letter? Out of some sort of misplaced guilt?

Jonas would never know for sure. His father's secret had died with him.

Although, it was possible to get Leon Tate's side of the story. Jonas hadn't personally experienced the outward disdain from Leon Tate, but that wouldn't stop him from attempting to confront the man, face-to-face. It would be nice to know exactly what his father was being accused of.

Jonas knew from the old photographs of his parents that he looked very much like his father. He and Jemma favored their father's coloring with blond hair and dark eyes, but Jazz and his other brothers, Jesse, Jacob, and Jeremy, had their mother's dark hair and light blue eyes.

Was the similarity between Justin and Jonas enough to knock Leon off balance? Maybe.

As Bella drove toward Battle Creek, Jonas called Jazz to fill her in on what Betty Cromwell had told them.

"No wonder Leon Tate hates us!" Jazz exclaimed. "I knew there had to be something more than just our last name bothering him. His daughter, Mary, obviously believes our father caused her aunt's death, too."

"It's weird finding out that our mom wasn't our dad's first love, isn't it?" Jonas mused. "Their marriage was always rock solid."

"First love doesn't mean anything," Jazz scoffed. "Jemma thought she loved her ex-husband, Randal Cunningham, but he proved to be a big jerk. Same thing with me and my former fiancé, Tom. He turned out to be a narcissistic crazy-man."

"I guess." Jonas couldn't explain why he was bothered by the letter and the story behind it. "I know you and Dalton are solid, but Jemma's happy with Garth, too, right?"

"Very," Jazz assured him. "No need to worry. And thankfully, Randal seems to have given up on his quest to sue for joint custody of Trey. Maybe because he knows Garth wouldn't put up with any of his shenanigans."

Jonas hadn't realized his sister's ex had threatened to sue for joint custody. "Good to know Garth has her back the way Dalton has yours."

"He'll do anything to protect her," Jazz agreed. "And I hit the jackpot with Dalton. Listen, thanks for the update, but I have to go. I'm meeting with the florist in a half hour. The wedding is only five days away!"

"Okay, I'll talk to you later." Jonas disconnected from the call and shoved his phone into his pocket.

"Why does it bother you that your dad may have loved someone before your mom?" Bella asked. "Your girlfriend left you, didn't she?"

"Yeah, but that was because I lost my leg." The words sounded ridiculous even to his own ears. "Or maybe a combination of the fact that she didn't really love me and I lost my leg. Who knows? It doesn't matter. You and Jazz are right. Our parents loved each other, and what happened before they found each other is in the past."

"For me, too," Bella agreed softly. "I lost Greg Wallace."

It took him a minute to realize she was referring to her fiancé who died while being deployed. "How long were you engaged?"

"We grew up together and were high school sweethearts." A sad smile played at the corner of her mouth. "We were friends long before we began dating, and being with him was comfortable and, at the time, felt right."

Hearing her talk about another man felt like gravel in the bottom of his shoe. Not at all comfortable. Then he realized what she'd said. "At the time?" he echoed, hoping his interest in hearing more wasn't too obvious.

She nodded. "After I heard he was killed in action, I felt a strange kind of relief intermixed with grief over losing him. I didn't tell anyone because it seemed so disloyal. But over time, I began to understand that I'd always miss Greg as a friend. He was very important to me. But deep down, I was relieved because I hadn't loved him enough to marry him."

Jonas reached over to take her hand in his. "I'm sorry for your loss, Bella. Greg sounds like a great guy. And even if you didn't want to marry him, that doesn't mean you didn't care about him."

"That's true," she admitted softly. She clung to his hand for a long moment, then released it. "I did care about Greg. He was my best friend."

It was on the tip of Jonas's tongue to offer to take

Greg's place as her best friend, but he managed to hold back. Especially since he didn't really want to be her friend.

He wanted more.

Jonas stared down at his lower limb prosthesis for a long moment. If anyone could handle his deformity, it was Bella. But she deserved someone better than him.

Steeling his resolve to stay away from Bella, no more kissing allowed, he closed his eyes and tried to rest. He'd have to be prepared for the hour-long therapy session that loomed ahead.

Sleep was impossible, but he must have dozed because two and a half hours later, Bella softly asked, "Jonas? Are you hungry? We're almost in Battle Creek and have time to grab something to eat."

"Huh?" He lifted his head and winced at the crick in his neck. "Sure. Let's stop for lunch. My treat."

Bella took the upcoming exit ramp that advertised a family restaurant less than a mile ahead. It wasn't quite noon, but based on the number of cars in the parking lot, the restaurant was doing brisk business.

Jonas was glad he was still wearing the prosthesis. Going out in public was easier when his deformed leg wasn't so obvious.

Thankfully, they didn't have to wait long for a table. Their server introduced herself as Sheri as she set two waters down.

"I'll have the chicken salad," Bella said.

"Make mine a hamburger."

"Anything to drink other than water?" Sheri asked.

"Not for me." Jonas glanced at Bella who shook her head.

"I'm fine, too." When Sheri left, Bella took a sip of her

water. "Are you thinking of sticking around in Battle Creek tonight? Or heading back to McNally Bay?"

He almost choked on his own water as the image of spending the night with Bella at her apartment flashed in his mind. As much as he wanted nothing more than to spend some time alone with her, he knew it wasn't smart.

He didn't have any willpower when it came to Bella Collins.

"My sister is expecting us back," he said, avoiding Bella's direct gaze. "But don't worry, I'll pay for your gas."

"I don't care about the gas," Bella countered. "I wanted to come along. Besides, I need to talk to my boss anyway."

That caught his attention. "What do you plan to discuss?"

Bella hesitated, then shrugged. "My resignation. Maybe that whole incident with the black SUV was nothing more than a freak accident, but it's not worth risking my life, or yours, for a stupid job." There was a brief silence before she added, "And I can't go back, regardless of the outcome of the investigation."

Jonas sat back in his seat, trying to think of something to say. "I hate that you're giving up your job over some arrogant surgeon."

"Yeah, well, I don't see another option." Bella lifted her chin. "Besides, there's a nursing shortage. I'll find another job."

Jonas knew she would, but that didn't change the fact that she was being blamed for something she didn't do. Hackbarth needed to take responsibility for his role in the patient's death.

Their food arrived, and they spent the next few minutes eating. Jonas kept an eye on his watch. He didn't want to be late for his therapy appointment.

When they finished eating, he swooped on the tab before Bella could react.

"Hey," she protested. "It was my idea to stop in the first place."

"My treat," he repeated. "Remember?"

She let out a huff but didn't pursue the argument. As they made their way to the door, three men came into the restaurant. Hampered by his crutches, Jonas wasn't able to move out of their way. A bald man with tattoos covering every inch of his skin rudely shoved him.

"Watch out," Bella said sharply. "You almost knocked him over."

"Who me?" The bald tattooed man leered at her. "Babe, you can do better than this lame duck."

Jonas flushed, it was agonizing to watch Bella stand up for him. Trained as a special ops soldier, he once would have been able to take on all three of these guys without breaking a sweat. But not now. He wished he hadn't left his Glock in the car, but he had. He swallowed his pride and tried to keep his temper in check. "Come on, Bella. Let's get out of here."

Instead of letting them pass, the bald tattooed guy stepped closer, blocking his way. Jonas instinctively straightened, staring him right in the eye. Bullies were the same everywhere, but this was the first time he'd encountered such obvious hatred since returning stateside.

"What's wrong with you, gimp?" Tattoo sneered. "You stupid enough to get your leg blown off?"

Jonas simply stared into Tattoo's hate-filled eyes, mentally preparing for the worst. "You really want to start something? You must like spending time in the clink."

Tattoo lashed out with his fist. Jonas let go of the crutches and used his forearm to block the blow. Pain rippled up his arm, but Tattoo's fist never met his face.

"Stop it!" Bella shouted. "I'm calling the police!"

Tattoo shoved past Jonas. Despite his efforts to stand on his two feet, Jonas lost his balance. Bella stepped forward in a quick attempt to catch him, but it was too late.

He crashed to the floor, his face red with embarrassment. Tattoo and his buddies laughed as they left the restaurant.

"Jonas! Here, let me help you."

He shook off Bella's hand. "Give me the crutches."

She handed them over, and he managed to get to his feet. The hostess came over, her expression clearly upset. "I'm so sorry. I called the police; they should be here soon."

"Doesn't matter." Jonas ignored the pain in his injured leg and moved toward the door.

"Jonas, wait." Bella hurried to catch up with him. He didn't look at her as he made his way toward the rental car. "You should press charges for assault."

"He didn't hit me." Jonas felt sick with the knowledge that if this had happened in another place, like outside of a restaurant, he wouldn't have been able to protect Bella from those goons. Even if he'd had his weapon handy, it wasn't easy to wield a gun at the same time as using crutches. "Let's go. I don't want to be late."

"That guy was such a jerk." Bella slid behind the wheel and started the car.

Jonas leaned forward, took his gun from the glove box, and placed it in his belt holster. He didn't say a word as she drove to the VA hospital. When they arrived, he got out of the car, took his crutches, and grabbed his backpack before finally looking at her. "Don't wait for me. I'm not going back to McNally Bay with you. I'll find a motel."

"I don't understand." Bella's expression was perplexed. "Are you upset with me?"

"No. I just need to be alone." Jonas quickly turned and walked away without looking back.

Knowing it was a pathetic way to say goodbye.

Bella swallowed a wave of frustration as she watched Jonas head toward the physical therapy gym. She wanted to run after him and force him to talk to her, but she let him go.

For now.

As she made her way inside the hospital, she thought about their encounter with the tattoo guy and his friends. Her heart ached for how Jonas must have felt, facing them with nothing more than his crutches and a prosthetic leg. And she was secretly glad he'd left the gun in the car.

She was impressed by how he'd blocked Tattoo's fist but knew that ending up on the floor, hearing their coarse laughter as they left had been humiliating.

Jonas didn't have anything to be embarrassed about. He'd acted appropriately, while those jerks had confronted him, looking for a fight.

The incident replayed over and over in her mind as she headed up to the third-floor surgical suites. Her boss, Jeff Greco, had an office adjacent to the locker room areas.

She knocked on his door and waited. After a few minutes, she decided he must be at a meeting. Seemed the managers were always being asked to attend meetings rather than spending time with the people who reported to them.

Realizing she should have written a resignation letter, she went into the locker room and found the staff lounge. Two surgical techs were chatting in there but quickly disappeared when she took a seat behind the computer.

Obviously she was still persona non grata around here. Which only reinforced she was making the right decision to resign.

Chrissy came into the break room, stopping abruptly when she saw Bella. "Oh, uh. Hi."

"Hi." Bella tried to ignore her friend's stilted attitude.

"Listen, I'm sorry about what happened," Chrissy finally said.

"Yeah, me, too." Bella knew she should cut Chrissy a break but kept her attention focused on the computer.

Chrissy left, and Bella knew their friendship was over. Typing up her resignation letter didn't take long. She kept it short and to the point. Bella printed the letter, then sent a copy to Jeff Greco and her personal email. After picking up the printed letter, she signed it and carried it back out to Jeff's office. She knocked again, but when he didn't answer, she slipped the letter under the door.

There. It was done. She stood for a moment, keenly feeling the loss of her job, her career, knowing she'd lost something precious. She'd wanted to help care for military vets as a tribute to her brother, Ryan, and to Greg.

Logically she knew she could still do that in another veteran's hospital, but walking away from Battle Creek left a gaping hole in her chest.

Enough with the melodrama, she told herself sternly. This was a job. People changed jobs all the time. No reason to get depressed over losing this one.

She turned and practically ran in to Jeff Greco.

"Oh. Hi." She hoped she didn't sound as flustered as she felt. "I, um, was looking for you."

Jeff was in his early fifties and had also been in the military. Navy, she thought, but couldn't say for certain. "You found me. Do you want to talk?"

His standoffish attitude wasn't new. He'd treated her like a leper from the moment the incident happened.

"Not really." She knew there was no point in rehashing things. "I slipped a resignation letter under your door."

His expression didn't change. "I see. Effective immediately?"

She arched a brow. "No, I gave my two weeks notice as required. But since I've been off the schedule anyway, I don't know if it matters. Up to you."

"I think it's best if we give you the rest of your vacation time to cover the two weeks." Jeff looked relieved. "I'll let human resources know."

Yeah, you do that, she thought sarcastically. She wanted to say something more but knew it was better to let it go.

Bella turned and headed toward the elevators. When she reached them, she changed her mind and took the stairs instead. Glancing back down the hallway, she noticed that Jeff had gone into his office, shutting the door behind him.

First Chrissy and now Jeff. Obviously it was time to move on.

The stairs led her to the main level of the hospital. She headed toward the parking structure. Thankfully, she had already cleaned out her locker after the medication error, so there was nothing else for her to take with her. It felt weird to leave the hospital knowing she'd never be back.

Outside, clouds gathered overhead an indication of the forecasted storm.

She quickened her pace, hoping to beat the rain when she heard her name.

"Bella."

The male voice sounded familiar, but instinctively she knew it wasn't Hackbarth. She turned to find Aaron Campbell, the surgical tech she'd worked with that fateful day.

The one who'd refused to back up her, claiming he didn't see anything.

"Hey, Aaron." She forced a smile.

"What are you doing here?" Aaron was a heavyset guy about ten years her senior, wearing jeans and a T-shirt with a lightweight jacket on. He moved closer, and she instinctively took a step backward as he was invading her personal space. She knew him, worked with him, but it wasn't like they were good friends.

They didn't hang out after work or anything.

"Nothing." She wasn't going to tell him she'd resigned, no doubt he'd blab to everyone in the OR, including Dr. Hackbarth. They'd find out soon enough.

"You spoke to Greco, didn't you? What did you tell him?" Aaron moved closer and pulled his hand out of the pocket of his jacket.

She froze when she saw he was holding a small gun.

"I quit my job," she blurted. What was Aaron doing with a gun? And what exactly was he accusing her of anyway? Her thoughts whirled with possibilities. Were all of these events— the brake line, the black SUV, the rattling of her door handle—all the work of Aaron Campbell?

If so, why?

"I handed Jeff my resignation letter, and he took it," she continued. "I swear that was the extent of our conversation."

"Keep walking," Aaron said.

"Where do you want to go?" Her blood ran cold at the thought of leaving the parking structure with Aaron Campbell.

"That way. See the black SUV over there? That's my car. Although now that I think about it, we should take yours. It's your new rental, isn't it? How convenient that you parked so close to mine."

The black SUV. She couldn't see the front of the vehicle but didn't doubt it was the same one that had rear-ended them on the interstate.

She tried to think of a way to stall for time. If only she'd gone back to the therapy gym to wait for Jonas.

"I don't understand. Why are you doing this?"

Aaron gestured for her to get into her rental car, but she waited for him to answer.

"Because it was me. I put the wrong antibiotic on the field, and I knew it was only a matter of time until you turned me in."

Bella gaped at him. "How could I turn you in when I didn't see you do anything?"

"It doesn't matter." Aaron waved the small gun. "Once you kill yourself, everyone will assume you were guilty all along and I'll be in the clear." His voice went hard. "Get in the car. *Now.*"

She tried to resist, purposefully dragging her heels over the paint on the ground, but when Aaron pushed the gun into her side, she gave in.

She opened the car door and slid into the driver's seat, fearing the worst.

By the time Jonas realized she was gone, she'd be dead.

CHAPTER FOURTEEN

Jonas wasn't surprised when Allan cut his therapy session short. The fall in the restaurant, in addition to the falls he'd taken at the old Stevenson house, had caused a blister to form on his left lower leg where it rubbed against the prosthesis. Every step he'd taken had been agonizing.

"I told you to take it slow," Allan admonished him. "If you stay off your prosthesis for a day, we can resume therapy on Wednesday."

Jonas nodded, unable to say much through his gritted teeth. The therapist was right. The most recent fall wasn't his fault, but he knew he'd overdone things over the weekend.

He took off his prosthesis and then crutched to the waiting room. He'd half expected her to be there, despite the way they'd parted earlier, but she wasn't.

The blame rested solely on his shoulders. He put his prosthesis in the backpack, then headed out to the parking garage, just in case she was waiting for him there. If she wasn't, he still had the key she'd given him on Friday. Maybe he'd head over to her apartment to see if he could catch up with her there.

Approaching the parking structure, he frowned when he saw what appeared to be Bella's rental car leaving the garage. He stopped, wondering if he was confused. He thought there had been two people in the car, not one.

But when he made his way to where they'd left the rental, he stared at the empty spot feeling sick to his stomach. There were scuff marks against the white paint that raised the hairs on the back of his neck. Was he overreacting? Maybe, but that didn't keep him from making his way back inside the hospital.

"Where is the security office located?"

"Down the hall and to the left," the helpful staff member told him.

He crutched as fast as he could, instinctively knowing time was of the essence. When he burst into the security office space, several guards jumped to their feet in alarm and reached for their radios.

"I have reason to believe a staff member was taken from the parking structure against her will," he said. "I need to see the video you have of the parking garage."

"You can't come in here demanding video," the older of the two guards protested.

"A staff nurse's life could be at stake." Jonas used every part of his military training to drill the two security guards with a steely glare. "Are you really going to risk her life over a few stupid rules?"

The two guards glanced at each other. Jonas wanted to scream at them to hurry, but finally the younger guard closest to him reached over to the center console and played with the controls.

"How long ago?" he asked.

"Not long. Ten minutes?" Jonas leaned over so he could see the screen better.

For several long agonizing seconds they stared at an empty parking lot. Jonas could hear the older guard speaking in a low voice, no doubt calling his supervisor.

"There!" Jonas pointed at the screen when Bella came into view. "Slow it down."

The guard fiddled with the controls, and the entire room went silent as they watched the scene play out. Jonas saw a second figure come into view, a heavyset male with dark hair.

"Can you tell me who that guy is?" he asked the guard.

"He looks familiar. I'll run a photo check through our computer system." The guard spun away to work a second computer.

Jonas watched the two figures on the screen walk toward Bella's rental vehicle. When it came time to get in, Bella resisted, and there was a brief struggle before she slid into the driver's seat. The male pointed a gun, and Jonas saw that Bella was holding her hands up in the air while the guy came over to get into the passenger seat.

A red haze of fury threatened to overwhelm him, but he did his best to maintain control. He looked over at the security guard scrolling through ID badge photos. "Try Aaron Campbell."

The guard typed in the name, and within seconds the photo popped up on the screen.

"I need his home address," Jonas said. "Hurry! Didn't you see that gun?"

"We need to call the police," the older guard who'd called for the supervisor piped up.

"Call them. But get me his address. And I need a vehicle."

"We have one that we use for security," the helpful younger guard said. He typed in another command, then nodded. "I got it. Campbell lives in the apartment building across the street."

The same building Bella lived in. "Let's go."

"Davy, you can't leave while you're on the job," the first guard protested.

"Campbell has a gun." Davy headed for the door, so Jonas quickly followed. "Send the cops to the apartment building."

Jonas was grateful for Davy's help. The security vehicle was parked close to the building, and Davy didn't waste any time in pulling out of the structure and heading for the building.

Jonas tried to think about why Campbell had taken Bella at gunpoint. So far the attempts against Bella had been designed to look like accidents. So where would he take her?

His gut told him Bella's apartment. He pulled his Glock from the backpack and secured it in the holster. When Davy pulled up in front of the building, he got out of the car as quickly as possible and grabbed his crutches. Davy was hot on his heels as he went inside.

With Bella's key in hand, he made it past the first security door. The elevator happened to be waiting, so he quickly went inside. Davy joined him, and they made it to the third floor.

He pulled his Glock off his belt holster, the weight feeling reassuring in his grip. Setting one of the crutches against the wall so he could keep his right hand free, he tossed the key to Davy and nodded toward the door. "Open it," he whispered.

Davy was all thumbs but managed to get the door open. He pushed it further, then eased through the opening.

The scene was something out of a horror film. Bella was crying as Campbell forced the gun into her hand and held it to her temple.

"It's got to look like a suicide, remember?" Campbell was saying over her sobs.

"No!" she cried.

Jonas didn't wait. "Drop the gun, Campbell, or I'll shoot!"

Aaron Campbell whirled to gape at him at the exact same time Bella kicked him in the groin. Campbell bent over, grunting in pain. Davy ran forward and tackled him to the ground.

"Watch the gun," Jonas shouted a mere second before a shot rang out.

"Davy! Are you all right?" Bella crawled over to check on the two men who were tangled on the floor. Davy lifted his head, then rolled off Campbell.

"Fine," he managed, lifting up the gun. "I wasn't hit, he was."

Sure enough, Campbell was bleeding from a bullet wound in his abdomen. Bella immediately lurched to her feet, grabbed a dishtowel off the kitchen counter, and pressed it against the wound.

"Call an ambulance," she directed.

Jonas caught her gaze and nodded. His fingers shook as he pulled out his cell phone to make the call. The sounds of police sirens grew louder, and he knew help was on the way.

Bella was safe. The danger was over.

He watched as she continued to provide first aid to the man who'd accosted her at gunpoint and realized in that moment just how much he loved her.

And even if it was the best thing for her, he didn't want to let her go.

~

Bella was so thankful to see Jonas, even though he was holding the dreadful gun.

"Don't let me die," Campbell begged as she held pressure on his abdominal wound.

Bella couldn't speak, still grappling with everything that had transpired

"She won't," Jonas said, approaching cautiously. "Despite the fact that you almost killed her."

"I—I'm sorry." Campbell was nearly crying now. "I couldn't afford to lose my job. I made a bad mistake at the last hospital I worked at, and I was afraid this time I'd never find another job."

"All of this was because you didn't want to lose your job?" Bella could barely comprehend what he was saying. "The brake line, trying to break into my apartment, rear-ending us on the freeway?"

He stared up at her guilt darkening his eyes.

"What about my job? What about the fact that you were going to KILL ME?" Her voice rose with a hint of hysteria, and Jonas dropped down to his knees beside her, putting a reassuring hand on her shoulder.

"Easy, Bella. He'll go to jail where he won't be able to hurt anyone ever again."

For the first time, Aaron Campbell seemed to realize how much trouble he was in. He tried to sit up, pushing Bella's hands away.

"You're not going anywhere," Jonas said. He placed his

hand in the center of the guy's chest and held him down. "Hear those sirens? They're coming for you."

Bella continued to hold pressure but leaned against Jonas, absorbing his strength. "How on earth did you find me?"

"Strong-armed Davy there to use the security video." The corner of Jonas's mouth quirked. "By the way, thanks for the key."

She let out a choked laugh, the horror of the past thirty minutes receding to the point that she didn't think she'd fall apart.

"Davy risked his job to save you," Jonas continued.

She glanced over at Davy. "Thank you," she said. "You and Jonas saved my life."

Davy looked a little embarrassed but nodded. "Anytime."

When the police arrived, it took a good two hours for each of them to tell their respective stories. The ambulance took Campbell back to the VA hospital accompanied by two different officers who'd cuffed his hands to the sides of the gurney.

When the last of the cops finally left, Bella grimaced at the blood stain on her carpet. Those moments that Aaron had forced the gun to her temple were the worst in her life. She could only imagine what soldiers like Ryan, Greg, and Jonas had suffered overseas.

"Hey, are you all right?" Jonas asked. His dark gaze was full of concern.

She forced a nod. "I know it's late, but I can't stay here. If you don't mind, I'd like to return to McNally Bay."

Jonas nodded. "Fine with me. But maybe you should let me drive."

She didn't argue. It was all she could do to hold herself

together. She was relieved the danger was over, but it had been a close call.

Too close.

She stared at Jonas's profile as he drove. Prior to his rushing to her rescue, and just in the nick of time, they'd parted in anger.

If she'd gone to the therapy waiting room, ignoring his demand to be left alone, Campbell wouldn't have had a chance to take her at gunpoint.

Useless to wish for the chance to do things over. She knew it was better to focus on the future. A future that she couldn't imagine without Jonas.

But how to convince him of that?

"I still don't understand how you found me so quickly. You should have still been in therapy."

"Allan cut it short because of my fall at the restaurant." Jonas glanced at her, flashing a wry grin. "Guess I owe Tattoo a thank-you."

She shook her head in amazement. How ironic that his most demoralizing moment had ultimately led to her rescue. She was quiet for a long moment before saying, "I thought I was going to die."

Jonas reached out to take her hand. "I'm sorry you had to go through that, Bella. It's my fault. I never should have pushed you away."

"I should have ignored you pushing me away," she countered. "I could have waited for you but didn't." She stared down at their clasped hands for a long moment. "Do you want to know what I regretted the most when I thought I was going to die?"

"No, what?"

She took a deep breath and let it out slowly. "I regretted the fact that I didn't tell you how much I love you."

Jonas jerked the wheel, clearly startled by her words. He abruptly took the next exit and pulled off on the side of the road. After throwing the gearshift into park, he turned in his seat to face her.

"What did you say?"

She smiled, gaining confidence in his stunned reaction. "I love you, Jonas. Every ornery inch of you. And I want you to know I don't expect anything in return, I understand it's too soon for you. There's no rush. I have to find another job anyway."

"Bella—I—are you sure?" Jonas looked truly perplexed. "You're so beautiful, so special, you could have any guy you want."

"Really?" She arched a brow and leaned closer. "That's good to hear, because I want you."

"Bella." Her name was a mix of frustration and prayer, but then he was kissing her as if he'd never stop.

She clutched his shoulders, wishing she never had to let go. But eventually they came up for air, and Bella began to laugh.

"Look at us? We're acting like a couple of teenagers." She waved a hand at the fogged-up windows. "We should head home."

"Home." Jonas lifted a hand to tuck a strand of hair behind her ear. "It's interesting you view McNally Bay as home."

She thought about that for a moment. "It's not just about McNally Bay," she finally said. "Don't get me wrong, it's a beautiful place. I love the lakeshore view, especially from the gazebo. But when I think of home, I think of being with you, Jonas. Wherever you are is home to me."

He pulled her close and kissed her again. "You can't keep

saying stuff like that, Bella," he said in a low husky tone. "Or we'll never get home."

She gave him a quick kiss, then settled back in the passenger seat. "You'd better drive, then. I think we might be able to get to the B and B in time for dinner."

Jonas started the car and headed back onto the interstate, quickly picking up speed. As the miles flew by, she tried not to dwell on the fact that he hadn't said he loved her, too. After all, they'd only known each other for a week. Might be best to cut the guy some slack.

"Bella?" Jonas broke the silence.

"Yes?" She turned to look at him.

"I love you very much."

It was as if he'd read her mind. "You don't have to say that just because I did," she protested.

He shook his head with a hint of frustration. "When I saw you helping to save that jerk's life after he nearly killed you, I knew I loved you. You deserve someone better, but I can't walk away. I love you, Bella. I hope you'll give me the chance to prove how much."

Tears pricked her eyes, and she reached for his hand. "I'll give you that chance, and more, Jonas."

"Good." He hesitated, then added, "You know, my sisters are going to be impossible when they hear the news."

She didn't follow. "I think they like me, and I know they want you to be happy."

"Are you seriously telling me you haven't noticed their matchmaking attempts?" Jonas asked incredulously. "They weren't subtle."

She laughed. "Okay, yes. I did notice. So what? It was sweet."

"So, I hate proving them right," Jonas continued. "After getting success with us, they're going to let loose on my brothers when they show up. I'm telling you, it's going to be full-on pandemonium."

"Are you seriously saying you won't enjoy watching them turn their tricks onto your brothers?" she asked with feigned innocence.

Jonas threw back his head and laughed. Bella thought his laughter was the best sound she'd ever heard.

EPILOGUE

Jonas held his head up high as he walked down the aisle with Bella toward the gazebo where Dalton waited. With Bella at his side, he didn't need crutches or canes.

They were partners, leaning on each other to get through each day.

Bella had suffered a mild form of PTSD after her close call with Aaron Campbell. Garth had let them know that her car had indeed been tampered with and that news, along with Aaron's confession was enough to put him away for a long time.

Jonas had been glad to be there for her. After the entire story about how Aaron had put the wrong antibiotic on the surgical field, her boss from the Battle Creek VA offered her the chance to return to her previous job, but she'd refused. Hackbarth had also called to apologize, and she'd reluctantly accepted his offer of writing a reference on her behalf. Which worked, as she just accepted a position at the Zablocki VA Hospital in Wisconsin.

Jonas applied for a position as a security guard at the

same hospital and had an interview coming up next week. He knew he needed to keep up his physical therapy if he wanted to land the job.

Painting brought him the peace he'd been searching for, but spending time with Bella was even more cathartic. Still, his best work of all was the portrait he'd done of Bella right here in the gazebo. Somehow, he'd managed to capture love shining from her eyes.

Love for him. All broken, bruised, and battered parts of him. He still couldn't believe his good fortune.

"You're so beautiful," he murmured as they took their seats in the front row on the bride's side of the gazebo.

"Thank you," she whispered back.

When the family was seated, including his brothers, Jemma and Garth walked down the aisle together, taking their positions as Best Man and Maid of Honor. Then Jazz came down the aisle with their oldest brother, Jake, who'd flown in from Ireland to be there. He'd arrived with a pretty brunette named Brianna Murphy, which of course had the family curious as to their relationship. Jazz's eyes locked on Dalton's, and Jonas thought he noticed a telltale dampness in Dalton's eyes as he gazed at his bride.

Jazz and Dalton's wedding ceremony was simple yet heartfelt. When it came time to exchange vows, Jazz went first.

"Dalton, I feel so blessed to have you in my life." Her voice broke, and Dalton tightened his grip on her hands to support her. "I promise to be faithful and honest as we share our lives together. I promise to always love you, no matter what life throws at us."

Dalton smiled when it was his turn. But then he dropped his head, then glanced out at the crowd gathered at the gazebo.

"I swear I memorized my vows, but the minute I saw Jazz, my mind went blank. No worries, I have a backup plan." He pulled his phone out of his tux pocket, which made everyone laugh.

Dalton glanced at his phone, put it back in his pocket, then took Jazz's hands again. "Jazzlyn, I wasn't looking for love or a family when I met you. I built walls around my heart, unwilling to let anyone in. You managed to bulldoze right past them, and I will be forever thankful for your stubborn determination. I promise to always love you and to put you and our family first in our lives."

There was a poignant silence before the officiant spoke up. "It's my pleasure to introduce Dalton and Jazz O'Brien. Dalton, you may kiss your bride."

Dalton drew Jazz close while the rest of their family and friends hooted and hollered. Jonas thought he'd never seen his sister so happy.

After the ceremony was over, Jonas sat on edge of the gazebo drawing Bella down next to him. She rested her head on his shoulder as they gazed out over the magnificent sunset dipping low over Lake Michigan.

It was difficult to fathom that he'd only known Bella for a little over a week. She was so much a part of him that he couldn't imagine his life without her.

He decided not to wait any longer. Taking the small ring case out of his pocket, he turned to face her. "Bella, I love you more than I can express with mere words. You've brought sunshine and laughter back into my life. Will you please marry me?"

"Oh, Jonas." She barely glanced at the ring, her blue gaze clinging to his, her hand resting over his heart. "Yes. Yes, Jonas, of course I'll marry you!"

He smiled and placed the small sapphire ring on the

fourth finger of her left hand, then drew her close for a long kiss.

"Jonas?" Bella asked when they finally came up for air.

"Yes?"

Bella smiled. "Would you mind if we got married here, at The McNallys' Bed and Breakfast gazebo? From the moment I arrived here as a guest, I felt as if I'd come home. Most of that is because of you and your family, not the structure itself. I know we can't live and work in McNally Bay, but I'd still love to get married here."

"I think Jazz and Jemma would be upset with us if we didn't," he assured her. "They love you like a sister."

"You have a wonderful family." Bella rested her head on his shoulder again.

"I love you, Bella," he whispered against her hair. "And home is wherever we are as long as we're together."

"I know." She put her hand over his heart again, and he covered it with his.

Together. For as long as they both shall live.

Dear Reader,

I hope you enjoyed *To Laugh*, the third book in my McNally Family Series. I wanted to highlight not just Jonas and Bella's story, but the siblings from previous books as well. I couldn't wait to give you a glimpse of Jazz and Dalton's wedding!

Reviews are very important to authors, so I hope you will take a moment to leave a review about *To Laugh* on whichever retail site you purchased the book from. I also love hearing from my readers and can be found at my website, www.laurascottbooks.com, or on Facebook Laura Scott Author or on Twitter @laurascottbooks.

The next book in the series is *To Honor*, featuring Jesse's story. I've included a sneak peek of the first chapter for your reading pleasure.

Sincerely,

Laura Scott

TO HONOR

J esse McNally headed into Daisy's Diner, enjoying the familiarity of the place. Daisy's hadn't changed over the past nine years since the last time he'd spent the summer at his grandparent's house with his siblings.

He'd been eighteen, nearly nineteen, and leaving for college in the fall at University of Wisconsin, Madison to study computer science. He hadn't returned to McNally Bay for any real length of time, other than the occasional visit over the holidays.

Until now.

Grandma and Grandpa McNally had passed away within three months of each other earlier in the year. His twin sisters, Jazz and Jemma, had turned their grandparents' mansion into a thriving new business, The McNallys' B&B. Jazz and Dalton had gotten married there this past weekend, their ceremony taking place in the white gazebo overlooking Lake Michigan.

Jesse decided to extend his visit for two weeks, needing a break after the recent and incredibly complex software restoration he'd managed for Avery and Arch Accounting. His firm, Software Solutions, had been contracted by the accounting firm to upgrade their security system after being subjected to a vicious attack of ransomware. After two months of working seven days a week, ten hours a day, he figured he deserved a break.

"Well, if it isn't Jesse McNally!" Betty Cromwell was the first to greet him when he walked in. She sat at a booth near the doorway, beaming up at him. "I'm happy to hear you decided to stick around for a while."

He grinned and bent down to give the town gossip a quick peck on the cheek. "You haven't changed a bit since the last time I saw you," he declared.

Betty giggled like a schoolgirl and waved her hand at him. "That doesn't mean much, since I just saw you Saturday at Jazz and Dalton's wedding." She lowered her voice to a conspiratorial tone. "You know, the only reason they're together is because of me."

"Really? How so?" It didn't surprise him that Betty Cromwell was taking credit for the wedding, but he hadn't heard the story of how Dalton and Jazz had met. The B&B had been fairly chaotic since all six siblings had been together for the first time in over a year.

"Dalton did some handyman work for me, repairing my bathroom, and I happened to mention how Jazz was renovating her grandparents' home on the lake. I encouraged him to visit Jazz as she may be willing to hire him to help with the construction project. He was a drifter at the time, you see, so I gave him a good reference. Jazz hired him." Betty nodded sagely, her gray curls dancing around her plump face, and spread her hands wide. "The rest is history!"

He chuckled. "I guess it is. I like Dalton; he does great

work. Did you see the garage apartment they built for
Jemma and Trey? It's amazing. And it's clear Dalton and Jazz
are very much in love."

"Well now, there's still time for the rest of you McNally
boys to find someone." Betty patted his arm. "Look at your
brother Jonas. He found Bella at The McNallys' Bed and
Breakfast, and now they're incredibly happy together."

Jesse nodded and tried not to roll his eyes. He liked Mrs.
Cromwell but wasn't interested in being the subject of her
not-so-subtle matchmaking. His girlfriend recently left him,
claiming she'd found someone else. Turned out to be a man
named Wade Nolan who didn't work long hours during software security breaches or travel from one company to the
next, providing computer expertise. Jesse wasn't exactly
heartbroken over Paula's breakup, but he wasn't looking to
get involved again either.

"No need to worry about me. I'm fine on my own, Ms.
Cromwell," he assured her.

As he spoke, a woman sitting three booths behind Betty
caught his eye. He stared in surprise as he recognized his
teenage crush, Carla Templeton. "Excuse me," he muttered,
leaving Mrs. Cromwell to move toward his teenage flame.

"Carla." He was shocked at the nervous squeak in his
voice and did his best to sound normal. "How are you?"

Carla looked up at him with a tight smile that didn't
reach her eyes. "Jesse. I heard you were in town for your
sister's wedding."

"Yeah, uh, wow. It's great to see you." His heart thudded
painfully against his ribs as he absorbed the fact that the
young girl he'd once loved had grown into a stunningly
beautiful woman. Her long auburn hair was pulled away
from her heart-shaped face, and her green eyes were as
bright as he remembered. Carla was still slender, yet

seemed to have gained more curves than when they were younger. It made him smile to remember how they used to sneak out after curfew to meet down at the lakefront. "It would be great to catch up. Mind if I join you?"

"Oh, I'm sorry, but you can't." She put her hand out as if to ward him off. "I'm meeting someone for lunch." Carla's expression turned wary as she glanced nervously over her shoulder. He thought it strange as the door to the diner was behind him, not her. "Listen, I only have a short break for lunch, then I need to get back to work. Please excuse me." She looked past him, lifting a hand to flag down the busy waitress.

"What can I get you, Carla?" A blond woman wearing a nametag that read Ashley plunked two glasses of water on the table, then pulled a notepad out of her apron pocket.

"We'll have the usual, thanks, Ashley." Carla looked at him one last time. "Enjoy your visit with your family."

The dismissive tone in Carla's voice put him on edge. A glance at the ring finger of her left hand confirmed she wasn't wearing an engagement or wedding ring, but that didn't necessarily mean anything. He wasn't sure where Carla worked, but it could be somewhere that didn't allow jewelry.

And what did he care anyway? It wasn't as if he was planning to move back to McNally Bay anytime soon. Their intense but brief bout of puppy love had burned out when they'd both gone their separate ways. He'd gone to the University in Madison, Wisconsin, while she'd been accepted at the University of Iowa.

Carla turned and rummaged in her purse, no doubt as a way to convince him to move along. It wasn't difficult to figure out she was meeting a man for lunch and didn't want or need him hanging around.

"Good to see you, Carla." He waited for her to acknowledge him before turning away.

"Take care, Jesse." She didn't meet his gaze and again glanced nervously over her shoulder. Maybe the guy joining her was in the restroom. Was she worried he'd start some sort of fight? Not hardly.

Disappointed, he moved away and looked for someplace to sit. Glancing at the counter, he noticed there was one open spot. He made his way toward the stool when a young girl who looked to be around eight or nine years old, with the same auburn hair as Carla's, came running toward the booth.

"Mom! Guess what? Daisy said I could earn some money walking her dog for her after school each day!"

Mom? Jesse frowned and watched as the girl slid into the seat across from Carla.

"She'll pay me five dollars to walk Bucky for an hour every day," the girl continued. "It's going to be awesome. I'm going to save up enough money to buy my own phone."

"That's great, Cassie." From where Jesse stood, he could tell Carla was shifting uncomfortably in her seat while studiously avoiding his gaze.

A sick feeling washed over him as he studied the girl. Her features were exactly like those of her mother, auburn hair, porcelain skin, and green eyes, but her gestures and mannerisms reminded him of Jazz.

He stared in shock. No. It couldn't be. Could it?

"Carla?" He hadn't realized he'd called her name out loud until she turned to look at him.

The guilt shadowing her green gaze was all it took. In that instant, he knew.

Cassie was his daughter.

NOOOO!

Carla's silent scream echoed in her mind as realization dawned in Jesse's eyes. In a heartbeat, he came toward them with a glint of fire in his eyes, and she did her best to ward him off with a narrow glare.

"I'm sorry, Jesse, but this isn't a good time." She managed to keep her voice level yet stern. "Maybe we could talk later?"

"When?" Jesse demanded as he loomed over her. She wanted to jump to her feet and push him back but knew that would only cause a scene.

As if they weren't making a scene already. Carla felt as if there were several pairs of curious eyes, including Betty Cromwell's, staring at them. News of this meeting was going to spread around town faster than flies swarmed fresh meat.

She'd never told anyone who Cassie's father was. Especially not her parents. Her father had been so upset upon finding out she was pregnant he'd slapped her across the face, screaming at her that the father better not be one of those no-good McNallys. Less than ten minutes later, he'd clutched his chest, going sweaty and pale. He'd crumpled to the floor while she'd called 911 and then began doing CPR. Her father had made it to the nearest hospital but had never woken up. He'd died a week later, leaving a heavy sense of guilt that lingered to this day.

"Mom? Is something wrong?" Cassie asked, picking up on the tension between the adults.

"Not at all." She tried to paste a smile on her face. She needed Jesse to pipe down or the entire town would know the truth before sundown. She glanced up at Jesse. "I get off work at eight o'clock tonight. We can talk then, okay?"

Jesse didn't look happy with the delay but too bad. There was nothing she could do to change it. She took over managing the grocery store a year ago, after her mom had been diagnosed with breast cancer. Meals with Cassie were the only indulgence she allowed herself these days.

And she wasn't about to let Jesse ruin this one.

"Fine," he finally agreed. "Where can I pick you up?"

She didn't want to admit she lived in the same house she'd grown up in. "I'll meet you at Gino's."

Jesse hesitated, then nodded curtly. His gaze lingered for a moment on Cassie, and she knew he wanted to be introduced. "Cass, this is an old friend of mine, Jesse McNally. Jesse, my daughter Cassandra."

"Hi." Cassie smiled up at him. "Do you live in the McNally Mansion?"

Cassie's blunt question caused Jesse's features to relax into a smile. "No, I live in Chicago, but my sister Jemma lives there. It's not a mansion anymore, though. It's a bed and breakfast."

"What's that?" Cassie asked, ever the curious one.

"Like a hotel, only the guests are offered free breakfast in the morning," Carla explained.

"Cool." Cass seemed to take the explanation in stride. "Nice to meet you, Mr. McNally."

"Please call me . . ." Jesse's voice trailed off, and he once again caught her gaze. She stiffened in her seat. There was no way in the world she was getting into this discussion now.

"You may call him Mr. Jesse," she said to her daughter.

"Okay. Bye, Mr. Jesse."

"Nice to meet you, Cassie." Jesse's eyes looked suspiciously moist as he turned away. Carla twisted her hands together under the table, trying to comprehend what had just happened.

She'd briefly considered leaving with Cassie for a few days while Jesse was in town, but July was the height of tourist season for McNally Bay, and the grocery store was exceptionally busy. Besides, she never expected Jesse would stick around long enough to run into her. Much less see Cassie.

But he had. And now he knew the truth. Even worse, it was clear he had no intention of leaving them alone.

She couldn't, wouldn't deal with this now. She took a sip of her water and eyed her daughter across the table. "So tell me, Cass, what kind of dog is Bucky?"

"He's a Goldendoodle, which means he's part golden retriever and part poodle," her daughter explained. "But not a small poodle, a big one. He has golden curly hair and is super friendly. Miss Daisy says he's a puppy with lots of energy, so I'm supposed to take him for really long walks each day."

"I see." Carla wasn't really thinking about Bucky as she toyed with her Cobb salad. Her appetite had vanished, and despite how she loved sharing meals with her daughter, her mind was already preoccupied with the upcoming confrontation with Jesse. The secret she'd carried for nine long years was about to come out in the worst way.

And there was nothing she could do to stop it.

Cassie eagerly dipped her breaded chicken strips in ketchup. "She said I can play with him during the summer any time I want."

"Hmm." Carla wondered what Jesse wanted out of this meeting. After all this time, did he really think he could just snap his fingers and become a father to their daughter? She didn't want or need his money. The grocery store was doing great, and she'd remained living with her mother out of convenience rather than for financial reasons. When Cassie had been younger, her mother had helped her out, babysitting and giving her a job. After her mother's six-month fight with breast cancer and chemo, their roles had reversed, and Carla was the one helping to take care of her mother.

"Mom? You're not listening."

"Uh?" She shot a guilty look at her daughter. "You're right, I'm sorry. I was distracted. What did you say?"

Cassie flashed an impish smile. "I said that Miss Daisy said I can bring Bucky home to live with us forever."

"Cass, you know that Miss Daisy only asked you to help with Bucky, not adopt him." She forced herself to take a bite of her salad.

"I know." Cassie was a good-natured kid. "Too bad Grandma's allergic to dogs or we could get one of our own."

"Just think, you'll get to have fun times with Bucky without the constant work of caring for him." The request for a dog wasn't anything new, and she was glad her daughter would be able to spend quality time with Bucky while earning a little money, too. Not for a phone, eight-year-old children were too young to have their own phones, but for something else.

"If Mr. Jesse is your friend, how come I haven't seen him before?" Cass asked.

She hesitated, caught off guard by the question. "I knew him a long time ago, before you were born. We haven't kept in touch over the years."

"Does he want to ask you out for a date, the way Mr. Thomas does?"

"No! Of course not. Where did you hear that?" She set down her fork, wondering how in the world Cassie had heard that her school principal, Dean Thomas, had asked her out on a date? They'd only had a cup of coffee, nothing more, and while Dean had made it clear he was interested, she couldn't find the enthusiasm to continue seeing him.

"Grandma told me." Cass popped a French fry in her mouth.

"Grandma has a big mouth." Her mother had made it clear that she wanted to see Carla happily married before she died. Not that her mother was going to die anytime soon. At her last checkup, the oncologist had deemed her cancer free. Still, it was annoying to know her mother had talked with her daughter about her love life.

Or lack thereof.

"We're just friends," Carla repeated firmly. "And you need to stop listening to Grandma. She's the one who wants a son-in-law. I'm too busy for that stuff."

Cass smiled, then frowned. "But, Mom, I don't want you to be alone either. And Grandma said you always push men off because you'd rather be alone."

It was disconcerting to hear her daughter talking about relationships. "Honey, trust me on this. When I find a man I can't live without, I'll marry him. Okay? Now let's change the subject."

Before either one of them could say anything more there was a loud crash from outside.

Diner patrons glanced at each other in confusion before looking through the windows to see what was going on in the small parking lot in front of the diner.

"Jesse. Isn't that your car?" Mrs. Cromwell asked in a loud voice.

Jesse jumped off his stool and strode toward the door. Carla craned her neck to watch as he approached a sporty red car. It looked like a Corvette, and she remembered how he'd always wanted a little red Corvette, just like the song.

She gasped when she noticed the windshield had a gaping hole in it. Jesse opened the passenger side door and pulled out a large brick. He hefted it in his hand and glanced around the area, as if trying to figure out who'd thrown it at his car.

She covered her mouth in horror. Someone had trashed Jesse McNally's car on purpose.

Who would do such a thing? And why?

www.ingramcontent.com/pod-product-compliance
Lightning Source LLC
Chambersburg PA
CBHW021018120726
47905CB00009B/3064